because you

have to:

a writing

life

JOAN FRANK

University of Notre Dame Press

Notre Dame, Indiana

Manufactured in the United States of America

Library of Congress Cataloging-in-Publication Data

Frank, Joan
Because you have to : a writing life / Joan Frank.
    p.   cm.
ISBN-13: 978-0-268-02893-0 (pbk. : alk. paper)
ISBN-10: 0-268-02893-1 (pbk. : alk. paper)
E-ISBN: 978-0-268-07976-5 (ebook)
1. Frank, Joan, 1949– 2. Authors, American—20th century—
Biography.   I. Title.
PS3606.R38Z46   2012
818'.5409—dc23
[B]

                                        2012019016

 This book is printed on recycled paper.

For Jack Pelletier, who started it all.

And for Deborah Mansergh Gardiner,
in loving memory.

If you can be happy doing something else, do it. Everything pays better. Everything is more honestly rewarded. But if you've got to do it, then you're a life-termer.

—W. D. Snodgrass

A mind is not given but makes itself, out of whatever is at hand and sticking tape—and is not a private possession but an offering. I had always had to write everything, no matter the subject, as if my life depended upon it. Of course—it does.

—Hortense Calisher, *Herself*

I think a big [advisory] you take from other writers, is courage— to go live your life as a writer, to believe in it, to go through what you're going to go through . . . That's enough, surely.

—Baron Wormser

If there is no wind, row.

—Latin proverb

Contents

Psychic Inroads, Scenic Routes, Culs-de-Sac

A Booth in the Marketplace

Reading

Making Art

Preface

Against All Odds

When you become a writer,
it changes you forever.
—Thaisa Frank

We live in a fast-forward world.

Media's avalanched our eyes and ears and, too often, our hearts. Speed and glitter, serving big profit, reshape our perception of the world to a kind of never-ending, NASCAR free-for-all. The phrases *a life of letters, a life of the mind, interiority*—these sound as fusty and obscure as old gramophone recordings. (Younger readers will stop here and look up *gramophone* on the internet dictionary.)

Paradoxically, there have probably never before existed so many books about writing. There are how-tos, step-by-steps, guarantors of fame and fortune or at least a robust second income. There are books (and periodicals and pricey software) advising on writing as a fulfilling hobby, diversion, or pastime, like starting an aquarium, cooking, or ham-radio operation. We find "survival guides." We also find a welter of very serious, smart books out there about craft and craft analysis.

I'm not interested in those.

My interest, in the pieces to follow, is in the emotional and physical and dream-life of writing (and reading) as an inescapable calling, and in ways of inhabiting that life. Writers write what they know, and many of the topics that follow pressed themselves deeply into my experience and, by consequence, my thinking. Yet they've often also struck me as screened off from the general dialogue, treated as unsavory—like that hidden little back room where the car salesman ducks away, to discuss your proposed purchase price with his "boss."

I wrote these essays in the grip of them, as serial obsessions. Some were published years ago in various journals; others are more recent. You will notice certain overlaps and repetitions, patterns revealing my own concerns and biases. You may notice that these biases suggest a quality of fanaticism: the determination to make art against all odds. These reflections are not meant to prescribe, though at times they may sound that way. They're meant to declare *here is how it has been for me*. My hope is they will form a coherent vision, one that may provide some communion. In the end, of course, a writing life is yours to invent. If you're a working writer you'll know this already. If you're just starting out, you must take it on faith (oh! as with so much else) that you'll find your way—that is, discover after a number of years that you've built the life piece by piece, without quite being aware of it.

Some of these essays focus on reading, which, for a writer, carries a slightly different weight than it may for others. Author Antonya Nelson once said that after you become a writer it changes forever the way you read, that a certain loss of innocence is involved, which is true. At the same time specific pleasures obtain, that might never have been grasped in prior innocence.

That trade-off would apply, I expect, to the life itself.

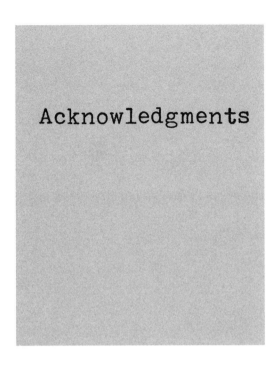

Acknowledgments

Sincere thanks to Robert Bly, Baron Wormser, and Thaisa Frank (no relation) for permission to quote from their writings and commentary.

Thanks to early readers Ianthe Brautigan, Bob Duxbury, Joann Kobin, and Jack Pelletier. Ongoing thanks to Bob Fogarty for unflagging support.

I am especially grateful to editor Stephen Little for patient diplomacy and guidance.

■ ■ ■

"Never Enough" was first published in *TriQuarterly Online*, a publication of Northwestern University (Winter 2010–11).

"A Hand in the Game: Reviewing" appeared in *Author* Magazine (July 2010).

"If You Really Want to Hear About It" appeared as a guest blog in *The Well-Read Donkey* for Kepler's Books, Palo Alto, Calif. (June 2010).

"The More We Typed, the Better We Felt" appeared in *Jabberwock Review* (Summer 2009).

"In Search of Heated Agreement" appeared in the *Antioch Review,* vol. 67, no. 2 (Spring 2009). © 2009 by the Antioch Review, Inc. Reprinted by permission of the editors.

"Gumby, Frankenstein, Jakob, Rosamund" appeared in *Center: A Journal of the Literary Arts* (Spring 2009).

"The Impenetrable Phenomenon" appeared in *Confrontation* (Spring 2002).

"Underwhelmed and Eccentric" appeared in *American Literary Review,* vol. 12, no. 1 (Spring 2001).

Special appreciation to the Association of Writers and Writing Programs (AWP) *Writer's Chronicle,* which published these pieces: "Revisiting Envy," vol. 32, no. 6 (May/Summer 2000); "The Stillness of Sleeping Birds," vol. 30, no. 5 (March/April 1998); "Imposed Yet Familiar: In Defense of the Memoir," vol. 30, no. 3 (Dec. 1997); and "To My Brothers and Sisters in the Rejection Business" in an early online edition of the *Writer's Chronicle.*

Madness
in
Method

Getting It Down

Few things have become harder to do at our moment of the new century, I think, than to think.

By thinking, I mean to sink, at a deliberate and comfortable pace, into the dense, measured, deep-roving consideration of all that has lately or long ago happened: all we've observed or read or felt or thought or done—what we'd perhaps like to do or think next, in result.

Writing is thinking on paper. And many writers undertake the craft in the first place because it allows them to *think their way through to* some new understanding or new question or problem— watch it unfold, feel it lead them, in the lines and paragraphs taking form before their eyes. It's a journey in the realest sense, often without a map. And despite the overwhelming, constant, clamorous interruptions of job, travel, family, friends and lovers, fatigue, depression, illness, all the relentless chores and emergencies of life—you do whatever you must to forge time to think and to write.

Since I became a writer, I've conducted an unscientific survey of how other writers manage to clear a space for their craft—ergo, to think. Most share the same woe: never enough time. They have to earn money, be parents and mates. They grapple with the old, old nightmare, the cake-and-eat-it riddle: they want to live, as well as to write. Old news—but when it happens to us, it feels new: this terrible battle of needs. Hair tearing—impossible to withdraw from one camp or the other. How quickly, too, it's over—one's life, I mean. And who amongst us has not examined her soul in the unforgiving hours, wondering what her mere existence might add up to?

Not everyone commiserates. Some seem to have the situation neatly pocketed (though these types raise my brows—Shakespeare reminds us that things are never what they seem). A teaching mentor during an MFA program once wrote to me, in calm response to my own bewildered longing for time:

"One has plenty of opportunities during the day to write."

I wondered, at the time, what on God's green earth he was talking about.

Was he mocking me? Should I start searching for some secret hidey-hole of time that I'd stupidly failed to see? I considered the source. This man, a venerable name among modern writers, taught and wrote. He'd written dozens of books in a popular genre, which I assume earned him bread-and-butter money. He wrote poems and short stories for perhaps less money—but he always wrote (or so it seemed to me) with the compulsion of his art. He had a wife who also brought in an income, and three growing children with all the usual growing-children needs. Therefore I had to assume he had contrived a schedule that gave him a living, while satisfying both his family (more or less, because families are insatiable) and his need for time. It must have been a schedule that enabled him to sink each day into that deep-duration time (thank you, Sven Birkerts) every writer so covets. I assumed that this man had mornings free to write—a very bottom-line yearning among writers. Free mornings, like any spoils of war, seem mainly to go to the unemployed, the retired, the already-wealthy, or those argonauts who've achieved *Oprah*-level recognition. Mornings tend to be our best hours—for clarity, energy, access to dreams. It's also most reliably the first portion of the day to be snatched away by the world.

Well, hurray for him, I thought. One can't waste time wondering where the hidden dues of an apparently perfect life may lurk. Each writer's choices for survival are assimilated from unique conditions. Though writers obsessively compare methods for getting it done, no one can really prescribe for another. We can *suggest* like mad, emulate, but rarely prescribe. Managing time is part of the authority we each finally have to grab for ourselves: no one will ever confer it. Perhaps all that writers can ultimately offer each other by way of ballast, consolation, or buttressing, is a kind of sympathetic witnessing: *I know it's hard. Keep going.*

Rougher therapy might borrow the blunt Nike slogan: *Just do it.*

     ▪   ▪   ▪

Compare my mentor's blasé comment with this rueful description by novelist Jane Hamilton, in her introduction to a directory of artists' colonies:

> Rilke said that in order to write he needed "unconfined solitude . . . (a daily routine) without duties, almost without external communication." As a mother and the wife of a farmer, those specifications for the writing life have alternately made me want to weep into a five-gallon drum and laugh my head off.
>
> For any artist, there is the profound problem of integrating the life of the imagination with the noise, the mess, the details, and the relationships of real life. . . . Whether an artist has a job or a family, or both, on top of the responsibilities to the artist's real work, there are always the incessant demands of the ordinary world.
>
> Without money for time and space, there were weeks, months, years when I had to hold that thought. And then, eons later, there was the bitter work of trying to find the

thought that had seemed important—No, that was important! Wasn't it?—on the scrap of paper, on my desk, in the bedroom, where there were also piles of laundry, bills to be paid, shoes to be taken to the repair. Better to look on the floor, where the scrap surely had fluttered among the dust and catalogs, unread books, last year's tax returns. . .

. . . It is not always easy to believe that our lone voices matter or are being heard in the modern age. Above all, what [an artists' colony] gives the artist, for the weeks or months we are staying, is the confidence that anything, all things are possible. If we are lucky, we carry that priceless feeling back to real life.

I found myself rereading this testimony with a rush of gratitude. *I haven't been crazy. It has been hard for others, too.* Sanity-bending, satire-defying hard. For some reason, though, it has traditionally seemed a hushed topic among writers, something averted by way of courtesy—lest you be considered a whiner, lest you perhaps somehow infect your listeners with the problem by speaking of it. Yet there it sits like the famous elephant in the room—a hairy, smelly one. And unless one disavows one's beloveds, or disavows eating and sleeping, it doesn't go away.

For years my late best friend and I traded ideas for how to deal with it. The amount of time and energy we gave to scheming was probably shameful. Get up an hour early. Stay up an hour late. Cut your hours at the office and accept a smaller paycheck. Sneak off to a secluded spot in the car at lunch hour. Park somewhere quiet on the way home for half an hour. Lie to friends and family and hide out somewhere. Take the laptop to a hotel (immediate problem—expense), very well then, to a remote corner of a library. I've turned off the phone, locked the doors, pulled the shades; I have indeed parked the car several blocks from home. Once I posted a sign on the front door: *Unavailable. Please leave a phone message.* (That offended a couple of people, but I don't hold with unannounced drop-ins in the first place.) My most precious steam-valve has been vacation time at a writers' colony for a couple of weeks. But at a ratio of two weeks to fifty, that's a lot of waiting. And in latter years I acquired a husband, who—go figure—feels zealous about taking vacation time together.

Author Heidi Julavits began writing in the kinds of secret spurts I practiced—but admitted it was hard to "write something narrative and linear [when] not living in either a narrative or a linear fashion at the time":

> Essentially I ran six years of controlled experiments on myself. And finally, I figured out, OK, I can't drink coffee, I can't write at home, I can't talk on the phone before I write. Things that you don't know until you're faced with trying to figure out how you work. I found that I can write about a thousand words a day, but not really more than that. . . . You have to figure out at what point you use up whatever gas you have, and [that] to push yourself any further just doesn't make any sense.

Julavits finally decided that she worked best by waitressing at night so her mornings would be free. Please know I am not recommending Julavits' solution. Nor, thank heaven, is she: "Figure out how you work," she writes, "and what you need to give yourself the time and emotional space to write. Then get a job that enables you to have that. That way, you're not under any pressure, and your life is set up so everything is complementary. Otherwise, I think writing can be very frustrating. It can become a thing that gets squeezed out of your life pretty easily."

I might mildly add that at the time this statement appeared Ms. Julavits was quite young. And though her advice is serenely logical, implementing it may prove, let us say, challenging.

❚   ❚   ❚

Since my youth, I've worked full time to earn a living. When I finally declared myself a writer I was a midlife bachelor, so for the first few years I could write without apology in any scrap of time around the job.

A pause now, to clarify a sore point: Unlike many writers, I chose to avoid teaching. No full-time teaching jobs existed in my area for people who didn't already have significant teaching experience. I knew I could not survive on part-time teaching—or part-time anything—in my high-rent region. Most crucially, I sensed that the profound demands of teaching would drain me of what I needed to make good writing: private, autonomous dream-time. Working for businesses having nothing to do with literary matters protected that privacy. If these day jobs punished me in other ways, they also never failed to provide a trove of material.

During those early, bachelor years, I wrote (or edited drafts) while doing yogic stretches on the living room carpet in the morning, a cup of coffee safely out of the way of bending and flexing limbs. I wrote against the steering wheel of the car at stoplights and in traffic jams. I jotted notes in bed at night before sleep, my tired legs propped on pillows, or when dreams woke me, or in that strange half-consciousness just before rising. Soon—with the terrible urgency of late arrival to the life—I learned to write in little blurts *during* the job whenever I could steal a few moments.

This practice has been a fraught, tense, treasonous business, and over many years I've refined it to a kind of double-agent ballet. I became expert at keeping papers turned facedown, flushing away whatever was on-screen the instant I felt anyone's approach. I developed such high-frequency body radar for people's footfalls— my hearing more acute than a hunting dog's—that when anyone did manage to surprise me I jumped so far as to cause them genuine horror. It took a while to calm my prickling adrenalin.

My jobs, usually front-desk positions, forced me to invent a rhythm of writing amidst perpetual interruption: the muscle for it (write-stop, write-stop) thickened and grew strong. It functioned like the hinge on a well-used cat door. I literally swung in and out, body, face, mind: from inside the writing on the screen and deep dream of it, the black dimensional cave of it—back out to the coworker needing help, the boss assigning a task, the insistent, bleating phone. That sound, added to the other demands, became a kind of hilarious torment. Hello, brring, brring, can I help you, brring, brring, certainly, no problem, brring, brring, I'll have it right back to you, brring, brring, brring, brring. My hands and arms flew from phone to desk to keyboard, like those of some many-armed Hindu goddess.

Somehow I actually got writing done in the midst of all this for the better part of twenty years—stories, essays, reviews, bits of novels. The experience made me a kind of quarterback for navigating the assaults of business life. I danced and sidestepped, karate-chopped and ploughed through them, smiling and quipping, clutching the precious writing dream to my chest like a baby held above the flood. My mission: to press the dream from heart through wrists and hands, into the keyboard and up to the computer screen before it (the dream) melted—before it evaporated—or as author Anne Lamott once horrifyingly phrased it, "I had a song, once." I learned to look people in the eye and make delightful noises at them while the essence of my mind operated light-years elsewhere. Most of the time I got away with it, though I didn't make many friends. It wasn't friends I was after. By day's or week's end I had a draft in hand to work with at home, evenings and weekends.

In this way I cobbled together a body of work.

When I moved in with a man with a ready-made family (and eventually, reader, I did marry him), the writing stakes shot past the ozone. Since then, the tug of war between love, art, and paycheck, described so ruefully by Jane Hamilton, has never relented. I live like a piece of malleable taffy between the demands of the beloveds, the business world, and the true work—the writing which craves long, silent hours. The bad joke, of course, is that writers must so often repudiate the world of the living in order to clear time and space to depict it. For those of us unable or unwilling to turn away too long from the living, the conflict feels as incessant, exhausting, and messily painful as the most disastrously risky adulterous affair.

When I was offered the first of the above-described office jobs many years ago, it also happened to be exactly the moment when I understood I had to begin writing in earnest. My parents were dead. There was no one left to offend, no one who'd try to stop me. I wavered, wondering whether I should not hold out for some more Julavits-like arrangement with paying work that would not directly interfere with writing. But I was too old by then to waitress or do a night hotel clerk stint. And lack of sleep would ruin thinking. I called my oldest friend, my high school English teacher, a patient coach and advocate who had urged me kindly but firmly at every turn to *write, damn it*. I worried aloud to Jack, on the phone, that I wasn't sure this new office job was the right thing to do; unsure it would allow me to advance the writing.

Jack thought a few moments. Then he spoke carefully:

"Well, Joan, at least you will be able to *get something down*."

Those words hit target. They urged me to become a good pirate, a creative thief, to throw time on its back like an alligator and write on its writhing underbelly when no one was looking. The words struck deep and held. I know I made an odd spectacle at the job, eyes riveted to the screen, responses dazed. Coworkers resented my puzzling elsewhereness, of course. They disliked the haze in my eyes, the delayed attention; I was not fully present for them, and this infuriates people like little else. I was accused of not being *proactive*. One colleague told me I'd erected a force field around my desk that effectively turned it into a bull pen.

I won't pretend the writing has not suffered. No matter how I enthuse about trapdoors and muscles, let's be clear: solitude, peace, and privacy are the holy of holies. No use pretending that silent, rested, solitary time, with velvet quiet and physical ease and no interruption or *threat* of interruption (almost as bad), has any relationship to the sort in which you sit in the midst of pandemonium, tensed and vibrating with dread of discovery or demands. I've known it both ways. I've worked at home, alone. I've worked in an isolated studio at colonies in Virginia, Vermont, and the New Hampshire woods (a total of five residencies in some twenty-five years). For all the rest of the time I've snuck out bits of work at home, evenings and weekends—and at the office. The difference between these scenarios is so stark as to feel—as it struck Jane Hamilton—tragicomic. Who knows how I might have written had I been cozy all those years in a calm room eight hours a day, say with a view onto woods or an empty beach, with someone leaving a basket of lunch outside the door and tiptoeing off—to work without my back and shoulders clenched? It doesn't take a behavioral scientist to surmise what's better for writing.

But. *I was getting something down.*

If it must be a bad version or no version, I'll take the bad.

Now: if the words *getting it down* became a mantra for me, I must also confess that from time to time I misplaced them. Often I felt crushed. My love for a few human beings and my ordinary need to pay bills seemed at times to cut away every last speck of access to writing—to trap me inside a culture that seemed fiendish in its ability to kill every attempt to rope off a few quiet hours.

Yet as we grow older, the aphorism *If not now, when?* no longer serves as some self-help cliché. It is knowledge that enters as physical fact.

One has plenty of opportunities during the day to write.

Perhaps my shrewd mentor was offering a mantra.

And maybe he was only saying, shut up and do it.

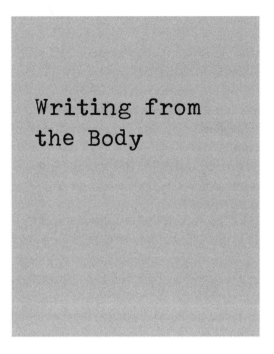

Writing from the Body

Presuming here shares the stage with making presumptions about sex. Unless one's a doctor or has just had a heart attack, one doesn't tell other people what to do with their own bodies (and even then, risks trouble). But a couple of things bear considering.

The brain is part of the body. (You'd be astonished how many people, particularly writers, willfully under-appreciate this.) The romance of Balzac's dying of caffeine poisoning, or of Dylan Thomas falling off his barstool after twenty-six whiskeys to expire on the White Horse floor, or of Fitzgerald and Agee and calamitous numbers of others drinking themselves to early ruin and death, no longer compels. Caring for health enhances odds for making good work, and possibly extends time on earth in which to make it. (Martin Amis: "Death is not a rumor.")

But there's something else: *the body informs the writing*. One remembers, imagines, and generates through the senses, as much as through ratiocination.

One of the passages in contemporary fiction that stands out for me is from Siri Hustvedt's lovely novel *The Sorrows of an American,* in which a mother is comforting her teenaged daughter following the girl's emotional breakdown (partly from having witnessed 9/11 firsthand). The mother embraces the girl almost an entire day as they talk, so intent on maintaining physical contact she keeps the girl's arms around her even while she makes sandwiches for them. I could see and feel this. Writing that matters is grounded in the body, in the life of the body.

Writing also comes from the body's thwarted life, or its differently-abled life—from trauma, damage, or illness. (In prior eras, it's been pointed out to me, one couldn't justly claim a writing vocation until one had first established oneself an invalid.) Proust would not have been Proust, we may argue, had he not been so hobbled by ailments that he confined himself, supine, to his famous padded room. The late Reynolds Price wrote from a wheelchair, as did the late Andre Dubus. Nancy Mairs has written memorably about living with multiple sclerosis. Some of our best work comes from the writer's struggle with the body, one's furious will to document its refusals, failings, and rarified needs. Perhaps the most wrenching and inspiring model is that of the late Jean Dominique Bauby, a magazine editor to whom remained, after a stroke, only the movement of his left eyelid: he blinked out the words through a special, invented alphabet, transcribed by a devoted nurse, that allowed the writing of his slender, excruciating memoir, *The Diving Bell and the Butterfly.* These exemplars, living and dead, inspire mindfulness and compassion.

I once read a slender tome called *On Having a Heart Attack,* by teacher and author William O'Rourke. He simply described the experience, which happened to him at age forty-five or so, all the way through to a quadruple-bypass operation. At book's end, without making any grand claims for himself, O'Rourke laid down a handful of sane guidelines, entitled "The List."

Everybody, he suggested, has a list.

One wants to live. One lives to make art. The body is the instrument.

Striving

Spit and Band-Aids

*The Business
of Art*

Recently mulling over the boxes and files of correspondence I've kept over the years, printed faxes or e-mails with my late best friend—a body of work that far outstrips that of any encyclopedia set or the Oxford English Dictionary or Joyce Carol Oates—I had a *frisson* of horror.

Those letters between us functioned as journals. Talking on paper or screen about reading and writing kept us alive—a secret oxygen tube enriching the thin air of day jobs and chores. We talked minimally of our own work, because we didn't want to jinx it. Instead we talked of what we were reading, of inspiring quotes from other writers, their work, their techniques and choices. We traded literary gossip and family problems and sympathy and advice, and lamented the usual gross offenders: a mad national culture, costs of living, assaults to writing time.

From time to time I had supposed that, down the road, scanning those reams of letters would teach me something.

But as soon as I began leafing through them this time, I understood suddenly that I did not need to look at them anymore to know their gists.

I saw with dismay that though I call myself an artist, the nature of my busy reports to my friend—consuming much of the day's best energy—were mainly those of a campaign strategist. I didn't fill those letters with gropings for the essence of truth or beauty or art. Nor, to my shame, did I spend page after page wrestling problems of craft.

Instead, those pages were about logistics. Arrangements. Schemes, plans, finagling. Trains, boats, planes. Money, money, money. Awards and rewards. Methods. Machinations. The politics of sneaking things through, firing things out, getting attention. Illnesses and medicines. How much sleep had been received, how much more was longed for. Loans and repayment schedules. What I could get by on. What I had to have.

To borrow the words of an old pop song: "Wishin', and hopin', and thinkin', and prayin'."

To borrow Saul Bellow's: "toil, tears, sweat and business-wriggling."

My letters, my thoughts, were about striving.

How wretched. How creepy; how low. Here is the writer in actuality: frantically searching for loan forms, wondering whether to go into debt to hire a publicist, watching bylines and reviews (and online social networks) to see who's doing what. Applying for residencies, grants, awards. Tearing her hair over money, agents, publishers, fellow writers, reviews, jobs, acceptances and rejections, page proofs, misalliances and misunderstandings. Getting sleep, getting time. Calculating, strategizing, kvetching.

Quotidian dreck. The spit and Band-Aids part of the writing life: yanking and knotting, bundling it together, trundling it along. The irresistible image is that of a one-man band, a different instrument attached to every limb as he marches. I would bet most writers feel caught, at some point, in some version of this. I would bet that very few are actually able to spend most of each day in a silent room at a peaceful desk with a single rose in the milk-glass vase, pen nub to creamy paper, sinking into the sacred dream. The rest of us belly-crawl along a ditch under bullet fire: tasks and errands, letters, forms, phone calls, faxes, e-mails, bulletins, favors. Responses, courtesies. Appointments. Queries, requests, proposals, counteroffers. Nudging. Application deadlines. Fund-raising. Readings. E-mail e-mail e-mail.

Have I mentioned earning a living yet? Have I mentioned family life?

And that's before anything's necessarily published. Once publication arrives there is publicity to seek, and if you get some, to manage it. Then, once you're considered established (or so I am told), people want you to blurb their books, judge contests, write recommendations, teach guest classes, attend seminars and panels.

Let's go back to the crawling part.

Bafflement occurs when we notice that we are nine-tenths given over to the busywork of writing, and one-tenth (if that) to writing itself. We had imagined that percentage to be reversed. We had imagined the job of writing to be contemplative. Interior. Sequestered.

Ah.

I'm confessing here that the greater part of my days is given over to the business end of writing, which to my mind means the *mongering* of it (as in fishmonger). Striving and conniving. And since I cannot change this, I wish I felt there was more merit in it.

There is only one merit: that of necessity. Simply, you do what you must to push the work into the world. A maniacal stage mother with her grumpy, sticky daughter.

Why? Because you long ago grasped that if *you* don't push it, no one will.

I'll repeat that for long-term storage: *If you don't, no one will.* No writing police will bash down your door at 4 a.m. demanding to publish (or publicize) you. It would be nice if that happened, and to some select few in the history of the universe, it does. The rest of us do Sisyphus duty.

As gentle consolation, I want here to remind those who feel stuck in striving, of the quality of company they're in. Read any great artist's letters, journals, interviews. Irrespective of that artist's brilliance, you will find familiar concerns. How to afford the next round of supplies. Whom to be jealous of. Whom to importune. Family dynamics. Appointments and rounds, needs and problems; speculation, longing, cadging and cajoling. Illness and enemies. Jealousy. Prospects. Funding. Self-pity. Pride, scorn, fear.

Trains, boats, planes.

Look at Mary McCarthy's letters, or Katherine Mansfield's. Chekhov's, Louise Bogan's, Thornton Wilder's. William Maxwell's to Frank O'Connor. I'm only tossing out names as they float past. Each *shlepped* through bewildering obstacles. Poverty, illness, peril. Rent, food, children, adultery, mental collapse, houses burning down. Getting the work seen and attended. Alcohol, drugs. Electroshock therapy. Bad romance, bad health, bad public relations.

Flannery O'Connor's early letters describe her struggle to dissolve her obligation to a publishing company which had first legal option on her first novel-in-progress, *Wise Blood*. That publisher wanted her to revise the novel to make it more pleasant, and she turned away this notion with calm but incredulous contempt. She was running out of money, trying to finish the novel and then work with the draft. She was also trying to sell a few short stories at the same time, and her distress—her sheer bafflement at finding herself in this *kind* of distress—are drolly evident in these letters. She was feeling as most writers must: *How did this happen?* How did I come to be spending so much time flailing in this sucking muck?

One review written about a book of Saul Bellow's letters speaks of Saul as being "deep in . . . 'the profundity game,' . . . constantly trying to balance the equation between rumination and action, solipsism and distraction, the temptations of selfhood and the noise of the real world."

At age 73, Katherine Anne Porter told an interviewer, "I think I've only spent about ten percent of my energies on writing. The other ninety percent went to keeping my head above water."

Vincent Van Gogh's letters to his beloved brother and sole supporter Theo bemoan the vagaries of the French postal system, worrying constantly about when Theo will send the next bit of money. With no funds, Vincent scarcely eats. He writes ardently of his work, of course. But right alongside that monumental quest, we find an obsessing that is more wrenching for its homely dailiness: Who might buy his work, and for how much. Windy weather makes dirt stick to the canvases when he paints outdoors. There is serious difficulty finding somewhere to live. A dismissive colleague berates his potential. Finding models is an ordeal, since he can pay almost nothing. Physical and mental breakdown, repulsed love, incalculable heartache. It is unbearably moving. Most of us, thank heaven, are not in such ghastly straits. But we can recognize, there as elsewhere, the unkillable insistence of the mundane.

One kinder truth about the routine business of writing is that it gives back a sense of guardianship and husbandry, the way farming or gardening can. When the fruits arrive, the gardener recalls the daily cost of coaxing them to life. Writing-related chores, even the most drudging, also generate a sense of continuity—evidence you've not deserted your own cause, even if you may not be producing every second.

That is my reasoning, anyway. It may not compel others. But it appears to me that task-tending threads us through the days, breaks the calendar into graspable increments, soothes as a jump-start and organizing principle. Even fire spotters must haul food and supplies, sweep the floor, and issue an occasional report.

Why do we bemoan the maintenance chores of a writing life? Here is how my late friend, Deborah, answered that: "I do think this spit and Band-Aids part of the writing life is not uncommon, even with successful writers. I read an interview with [Kazuo] Ishiguro wherein the interviewer was allotted fifteen minutes of interview time while Ishiguro was walking to another appointment, and you got such a sense of the nightmare of packed time and no time to walk, and Ishiguro apologetic and under the thumb of his editor who scheduled him."

Much, she reminded me, depends on a writer's attitude toward getting published. "I don't know who gets to have a 'true' writing life except for the fabulously successful or for the hermit who doesn't care about publication. I actually know a man who got a job as a park ranger in a remote part of the country and who went for ten years of his life without speaking to a soul except on a ham radio as part of his job and who wrote pages and pages of poetry which he never sent anywhere. And he said those were the very best ten years of his life. And I believe him."

My friend also reminded me that successful writers tell interviewers they write every day from nine to five, sometimes evenings. The less famous declare they write every day before the kids wake up, on Sundays, during summer, or at art colonies. Her point, I think—and it seems to be something one must relearn repeatedly—was that you square off with it to get it done however you can. That's what striving figures into: doing what you can within the life you choose—more accurately, the life that chooses you.

Here is Katherine Anne Porter: "I think probably the important thing is to get your work done [any] way you can—and we all have our different and separate ways. But . . . I believe that if you misuse [art] or abuse it, it will leave you. It is not a thing that you can nail down and use as you want. You have to let it use you, too."

I'll go back to those boxes of letters, I think, when I'm much older. Seeing them then may teach me something that's not so obvious yet. I am guessing I'll be touched by all that terrible urgency.

The Stillness of
Sleeping Birds

In her enchanting book of meditations on the act of reading, *Ruined by Reading*, author Lynne Sharon Schwartz describes, among reading's many mysterious pleasures, the option of sitting alone, "reading uninterrupted to my heart's content"—and my attention stops there.

When I first read those lines, years ago, I endured a long, jostly bus commute to an office job. Brown hills rippled alongside like a movie backdrop; young men boasted and swore cheerfully a few seats behind me; the soft hiss of someone's iPod floated over the grind of bus engines; colognes comingled. Those usual distractions faded as I stopped dead at the word in Schwartz's sentence, sounding it in my reading ear:

Uninterrupted.

I remember hunching closer to the pages.

Schwartz tells how as a girl of ten, in the midst of mulling a poem of Keats's, she was called away summarily for a visit to relatives:

It may have been from that moment that I contracted a phobia for which there is no name, the fear of being interrupted. (It may also be why, as I grew up, I came to prefer reading late at night, when the intrusive world has gone to bed.) Sometimes at the peak of intoxicating pleasures, I am visited by a panic: the phone or doorbell will ring, someone will need me or demand that I do something. Of course I needn't answer or oblige, but that is beside the point. The spell will have been broken. In fact the spell has already been broken. The panic itself is the interruption. I have interrupted myself. Oddly enough, very often the phone does ring, just as paranoiacs can have enemies. Life is designed to thwart ecstasy; whether we do it for ourselves or something does it for us is a minor issue.

I know that phobia. News? Hardly. But because of my *menage à plusieurs,* I have lived many years with the anguish of constant interruption.

The word looks like it means *come between and tear.* And so it does. Dreaming before lines of words on the computer screen, I am also gazing a dimension further—at my own mental screen, on which grainy images try themselves. Each time the tissue of these diaphanous ideas begins to build, each cell of conceived thought knitting up the next, a tender ligament between the mind and its vision begins to form.

This period is akin to what author Sven Birkerts has called "deep-duration time," a mysterious state in which readers slip outside present time and "bustle about" in their mind's eyes, building the world of the book. Similarly, Schwartz describes her older sister immersed in reading, demonstrating an enviable quality of willed deafness: "My sister appeared to be present, but she was in the book. This is a great and useful gift. The stunned petitioner retreats, daunted by an invisible power that can drown out the world."

I would suggest that, for a writer, Birkerts' term connotes a similar trance, that dense ether in which we transcribe fragile dreams onto the page. While in this state we have little or no truck with the apparent world or chronological time. Actual days and nights can melt away, and we may have felt no sense of their passing. It looks arrogant, even pathological. Yet we are likely to feel magically replenished on return from deep duration time—especially if we can float back to the present at an unforced pace.

Instead, shock rouses us: the knock at the door, the buzzing or singing phone; someone arrives, someone needs—timed as if deliberately to shatter the critical moment, the moment of stepping into the dreamscape as images sparkle shyly into view, begin to move and to speak. Then the knock, the doorbell or phone, the chime of e-mail. Our eyes fill suddenly with black stars, as if rubbed too hard.

That's when I turn toward the intruder, struggling to compose my face, pulling my gaze from the screen or pages so clumsily I fancy any observer can see the slow, stupid reconfiguration of my features. Even my voice wobbles until I've fully returned from what Georgia O'Keeffe once called "The Great Far Away." I attend the need—the child's, coworker's, spouse's, friend's, people who mean no harm and have no sense of trespass—praying to retain anything of what I heard and saw before the whole thing was razed. Then I begin again, trying to attach torn shreds, to build upon them. In this way I have fashioned a jerky form of a writing life—a body of work—and become a woman in a constant state of a kind of dazed inflammation.

I have a little studio at home, where I scuttle whenever I have some minutes. I write in snatches at work—anything to get the writing out. As Francine Prose noted when her students complained they could not find time to write: "There's *never* a good time. If you only have fifteen minutes, use the fifteen minutes." And Gail Godwin wrote, "Write when very tired."

Jane Smiley once told an interviewer, "Yes, I let the children in [to my studio] while I am working. Why not? It's possible they may give me something I can use." And I recognize the impulse that led her to say this, a greed-coated pragmatism, as well as a chemistry experiment: to mix odd elements and see what foams up. It's an attitude I try to remember when I smile at my family and friends as they come and go, while I greet and embrace and tend to them. But the terrible fatigue of interruption grinds me down.

It is not that whatever I may have produced without interference would have proved some brilliant milestone. It is rather that I starve for the unpunctured state itself, the tonic of stillness, of unbroken dreaming. Static on surface (sitting and twisting a pinch of hair, staring out the window or off to a cobwebbed corner), the *internal* mechanics work like those of breathing to deepest capacity, saturating psyche and soul with a renewed power of autonomous clarity.

A roundness of thought: that is what interruption tears at, claws up.

In reading or writing we imagine with free-ranging motion, escaping present-time constructs—a process which nourishes and restores us in ways we don't yet fully understand, much like sleep. If someone or something repeatedly stops that wide-ranging movement midway (or even earlier), the "muscles" for this function learn to *anticipate* the siege—to expect the abrupt wall they're about to slam into. They adapt (as I see it) by tensing: strong for the brief allotted portion of their potential span, but halting in Pavlovian reflex at precisely the position of customary stoppedness, of expected interference. What happens then to our ability to think deeper, larger, more audaciously? What do you call a state of mind which anticipates its own recurring annihilation?

▮   ▮   ▮

Even if I were not so personally immersed in the problem of getting enough stillness for writing and reading, I would feel uneasy in a culture that worships speed and distraction—these are interruption's henchmen. As Charles Baxter laments in his wonderful essay on the quality of stillness in fiction, "velocity understood in relation to action and language, has been throughout this century one of those ideological headaches that will not go away. The peculiar and immeasurable speed of . . . information is a special problem of the twentieth century . . . resulting [in] data-nausea and information sickness [that] are probably unique, at least on a mass scale, to our time."

Speed of information bombardment disallows dwelling, disallows sinking deep. It is interruption at Star Wars levels. We refine and exalt it, and it shrinks our options for unmolested real time: cellphones, texting, pagers, the internet and e-commerce, news and film flashes, fast, faster, fastest. A television commercial for a brand of minivan some years ago showed an American family racing fast-forward through its day in the car, a child screaming with pleasure from the backseat as the narrating voiceover proclaimed that life got faster—therefore, better. In such a climate, the writer or reader begging to be left alone to dawdle and dream appears as dense an archaism as a dinosaur nosing the edge of the tar pit.

Sometimes I am myself the speed monger, cutting off or cutting in or cutting away. Angry or impatient or tired, inflamed by barred access to stillness, I rip through daily functions in a fury— against the resistance of objects, the slowness of traffic, the congealing vagueness of the very elderly. My husband claims I even look at pictures in art galleries too quickly. But that is often because I know he has already absorbed them at his own leisure in prior visits—he takes his classes to galleries—and is waiting for me, trying to be patient. Knowing people wait for us, whether they wait kindly or angrily, confers interruption of a subtler kind, the slow seepage of our own guilt into the time "stolen" from someone else.

One morning in early fall I went running in my neighborhood before sunrise. Stars glittered in the waning night and straight before me rose an arcing meteor, its tail a fan-shaped wash of light. I'd never have seen it had I not been there just then. But what especially set this predawn hour apart (which I finally managed to identify) was that there was no sound. No birds had yet waked. Since birdsong is typically a glorious herald of mornings where I live, it was a sound of its own, the stillness of sleeping birds—and why would I wish to shatter it by filling my ears with iPod noise? This too would come between and tear.

As Baxter notes in his essay:

What's remarkable is the degree to which Americans have distrusted silence and its parent condition, stillness. In this country, silence is often associated with madness, mooncalfing, woolgathering, laziness, hostility, and stupidity. Stillness is regularly associated with death. This distrust of silence and stillness comes to us as a form of muddleheaded late Puritanism, which looks upon idle hands as the devil's playground, and silence, like Hester Prynne's silence, as privatized rebellion, a refusal to join the team.

The daydreaming child, or daydreaming adult, is usually an object of contempt or therapy. Vitality in our culture, by contrast, has everything to do with speed and talk.

Speed and talk collude to create distraction, in its most intricate forms, from the terror of stillness. I cannot dispute anyone's access to limitless distraction, which Americans seem to claim as a civil right: purposeful interruptions, chosen perhaps to alleviate thoughts (or a lack of them) that we cannot bear. At times I have resorted, as most of us have, to one or another gross distraction. During a lonely period in my early thirties—before I began writing in earnest—I remember switching on the television as soon as I arrived home from work the way people of earlier eras lit a good fire, and kept the thing on until I slept. It quacked and burbled in the background like an antic vital sign.

▌   ▌   ▌

I am trying to read a short Sunday newspaper piece at the kitchen table. My husband also reads across the table, but he stops his reading to comment to me. I make acknowledging noises and smile and refocus on my page, hoping he will be drawn into the section before him. He speaks again. I make the same noises and resume the same sentence I am reading. We have so little time together I cannot bring myself to utter, "Sweetheart, please, I need to finish this." Because if I had my way I would always need to finish something, always need to be alone. If I achieved that—and the option to live alone again is always available, after all—I could not bear it. I love my husband, my family. Therein, the paradox.

For if you take away unstructured, deep-dream time you flatten and stunt perception and with it a rounded sense of narrative, of belief in the dimensional story-in-motion. As goes belief, so goes meaning; so goes possibility. The world and its complicated riches shrink away. See little, expect less. Words become glib and utilitarian: whatever zips us there fastest. What might have been revealed to us even fleetingly during our short, puzzling lives may be forever lost.

Refuges exist, of course. Art colonies provide blissful periods of solitude and space, but time spent at them is more difficult to achieve the older and more entrenched (family-rearing, wage-earning) one becomes. In usual fact, few of us have the money to buy necessary pockets of stillness, and our most patient mates and friends may become fed up with that diabolical other lover who demands every drop of extra time: art. "Most women can manage two out of three (love, wage earning, art) but not all three," my late best friend once suggested, and daily I try with all my strength to disprove this, and daily pay the price: more than simple fatigue, a kind of compounded grief for the recurring blackout, the long intervals of barred access to myself, access to "a quality of mind and discernment, a rarefied focusing," as Schwartz calls the act of writing.

Listen to Raymond Chandler, during a period when he was writing for Hollywood: "I have a sense of exile from thought, a nostalgia of the quiet room and the balanced mind. I am a writer, and there comes a time when that which I write has to belong to me, has to be written alone and in silence with no one looking over my shoulder. . . . It doesn't have to be great writing, it doesn't even have to be terribly good. It just has to be mine."

But there's another kind of exile: that of standing outside life's warm windows looking in, something I knew quite well during many years of bachelorhood. And though I accomplished much work during those years—pure dreamtime—I interrupted it myself with panic about a different poverty: that of missing human communion. And here's the damnable thing: too much communion enervates for its inevitable banality! Our responses to each other, however deeply felt or reasoned, however intimate, organized as a series of outward gestures—if for no other reason than that we inhabit discrete bodies—must share language. Interiority waits for solitude.

Yet when that communion with other humans is withheld completely, most of us begin to starve for what quickly, even accusingly, looms to us as the stuff of life. Papers and words would seem ash-cold if they had to serve as our only comfort. Don't mistake me—art can never be bad company, except perhaps as the sole substitute for its living subject: us. Complete withdrawal still strikes me as something like memorizing instruction manuals while the splendid, gleaming machine rots away, untried, in storage. Think too of Chekhov's characters in Moscow who pine for the country: once installed in the pastoral *dacha* they immediately yearn for the sophistication and vigor of Moscow. The balance between engagement and seclusion, between presenting to others and solitary stillness, is elusive; the craving for that balance, riddling—and unstoppable.

Be Careful Whom You Tell

It is very tempting—and for one or two seconds, deeply satisfying—to tell people you are a writer.

In the next beat, you may be very sorry you uttered a word.

Here are some typical responses from the world at large:

Really? I do some writing, myself.

Is the novel fiction?

Have I heard of you?

Say, I have the perfect idea for a book (story, article) you should write. Let me tell you about it.

Have you tried getting on Oprah?

Why don't you write the sort of stuff that what's her name writes, the one who's famous? That's all you need to do. Then when you're rich, you can write whatever you want.

Gee, I just love that book about the funny dog. You know the book I mean?

Hey, I wonder whether you'd have a look at this thing I've been working on. Just tell me what it needs, and then whatever I need to do to get it published.

Trying to steer through these cheerful rejoinders can sink the toughest of us into a swamp of polite lies, defensiveness, shame, doubt, anger, even depression. When people assume that writing is something done for fun, and maybe a little profit on the side (like crocheting beer-can hats) or, conversely, that it is done to make a killing; when they brightly ask you to name one of your products that they might recognize—you've got some serious hurdles to jump.

Social acquaintances who know that you write will ask every single time they see you, with a mischievous twinkle, *how's the writing going?* This is often code for *have you amounted to anything yet?* Again, they may also insist you hear out their latest idea for a book or story. They may even suggest, jokingly yet with an edgy glint, what their cut of your anticipated gross should be, for having passed along their idea. If you try to describe the fact that you're presently struggling (to get a story taken, to find a publisher, to find an agent, to find a new agent, etc.), their hiked brows will indicate their thoughts: *Hey, I already gave you the greatest tip of your life. All you had to do was write a best seller like what's her name's. Your problems would be over now.*

If you tell people you write stories that have "only" appeared in literary reviews (because odds are stupendous no one's heard of these, let alone read one), a strange, default humiliation pools up. The American implication always bearing down is, if you're not famous or rich, how can you matter? If you tell people you've got a new book out this minute, or even many books, and your listeners have never heard of you or your books, that's another spritz-in-the-eye. Though you know rationally that public reaction should be the least of your worries, you may have to do some deep breathing in these moments. Few people recognize the names of this year's National Book Awards or Pulitzer or even Nobel winners. (*I* don't often recognize them.) Yet the sense of desolation, of invisibility, of an absurd futility that creeps like toxic gas into a writer's conscience when people stare blankly at her, is real.

Be especially wary at the day job. Those worlds that function well apart from the literary circuit, particularly those that dispense a regular paycheck, are better left in virginal innocence. Not for nothing, not *from* nothing, came Joyce's slogan "silence, exile, and cunning." If day-job bosses learn that you write, they may immediately suspect you of tapping away at the Great American Novel on company time—which may certainly be true, but certainly not for them to know. It's tempting to want to tell coworkers. When you win an award or receive an acceptance, you long to shout, to run from cubicle to cubicle buttonholing your pals with the magical news. *Resist that impulse with all your might.* Colleagues' apparent joy can turn around to bite you.

The human psyche is a complex apparatus. Awful stuff may be set in motion, internally, with another's success. No one wants to feel handled—and day-job coworkers may suddenly feel handled when they hear of your publishing victory, even though you've deputized them as a confidante in your special secret, and even though they've sworn they've been cheering for you. More treacherously, a hierarchy of meaning may suddenly invert for them. No one wants to feel peripheral, or mere, in his own sights—not even by remotest inference. "Thinking about your next book?" one boss asked testily, when he caught me in a pensive expression at my desk. This was the same man who'd asked my advice in coaching his teenaged daughter, who "was interested in writing."

Coworkers' lopsided perceptions of the nature of the gig can also be unintentionally comical. When I gave a reading from a new novel in my hometown a few years ago, I decided to risk inviting all the sympathetic employees at my office. They happened to be civil engineers. They made excellent money. (They drive nice cars, take lavish vacations—surely they would buy a book.) A group of them showed up at the bookstore, men and women, young and middle-aged, some toting husbands and wives. They smiled jubilantly at me on arrival, sat down balancing their tea and cookies, listened to my words carefully, even asked a question or two. And when the applause died down after the reading, they sprang up and marched out of that store. It took me a little time to figure it out: they didn't understand that to show full support for a writer-friend, *you buy a book*. They believed they'd done their duty, like going to church.

They'd just managed to duck out before the passing of the offering plate.

❚   ❚   ❚

Americans tend to feel uneasy when confronted with someone professing to practice art—or for that matter, anything sounding high-minded. We distrust and fear what we haven't directly experienced, because we don't wish our ignorance to be exposed. An editor I once knew in a software publishing firm, a shy, unpresuming young woman, introduced her young husband at a company holiday dinner as an astrophysicist. All giddy cocktail-chitter was struck mute. People stared at each other. How to respond?

More complicated reasons may lead to some bafflingly hostile reactions. People may mock your seriousness or your skill or qualifications, or the art form, or even, perversely, the non-culture which ignores the art form. They may offer bitter or ironic or melancholic comments which may seem to wish to defeat or discount you. Sometimes they just smirk, a kind of wild fury in their eyes. (My dentist reacted this way. Terrified, I made sure from then on to mention only weather and family. Only much later did I learn that he'd once been a classical pianist.) Often, people use sharp remarks to defend against invisible demons that pop up inside them when they hear of someone else's passion—demons accusing them of insufficient risk, meaning, or passion in their own lives.

A related issue—and a terrible trap I would urge any writer in any stage of development to avoid at all costs—is the serenely sweet question, *What's it about?*

I insist, from long observation, that there is no way that *any* answer to this question will satisfy anyone. None. Whatever you say will fall short. People's faces will widen with puzzlement or disappointment. Far worse—and you've heard this elsewhere, perhaps many times, but I have felt its truth—if you talk about work in progress, you may lose the mysterious energy of the dream that propels it. If you cherish that energy—and for heaven's sake, it's everything—shut up. Explain quietly to those who ask: "I'm in the middle of something new, and that's all I can really tell you right now." And if people press you for its subject or setting or era, or even the genre of the damn thing, no matter how much wine you've drunk or how tenderly you regard the person asking, hold fast. Smile as sweetly as you can and say: "I'm sorry—but I'm superstitious about talking about work in progress. When it's done I'll be happy to pass it your way. In fact I'll invite you to the reading!" Questioners may shrug or look crestfallen, but believe me—that's nothing, nothing compared to the vacant dismay you'll watch their faces assume after you've told them what your book is about or what happens in it.

Acerbic author Fran Leibowitz once pointed out that the occupation of writing is tantamount these days, in terms of archaism in public perception, to that of sheepherding or horseshoeing. Even the biggest literary names, alive or dead, will mean little or nothing to most citizens. After a time, one accepts this.

One also does well to remember that one mentions one's passion at one's peril.

Maybe it was never really otherwise. Imagine Shakespeare's lot—rotten vegetables thrown, or worse—and so on. Perhaps you have to stay within the boundaries of a bookstore or college campus to speak of your work with any ease. But in those domains, alas, different hostilities may assail you: professional jealousies, nostalgia, world weariness. I remember bravely answering a famous fiction writer who asked, many years ago at a cocktail party—he was one of the crown-jewel authors of a famous university—that I, too, was a fiction writer.

"Yes," he sighed, exhaling cigarette smoke.

The word sank through the air like the smoke from his lungs, his baggy eyes scanning the middle distance with inexpressible exhaustion. I remember feeling sick. No doubt he had every reason to feel as he did. Likely he'd taught too long. His health was bad (he died a few years later). Likely he longed to return to an unfinished project, or several of them. But all the compassion in the world couldn't mitigate my sense of what was before me: that this man would just as soon peel off his own skin as hear the words "fiction writer" again. In the end I had to decide that this famous writer's unspeakable fatigue could not annul my calling, or at least my shot at it. I couldn't allow that. I didn't begrudge him his life and success, but I couldn't erase myself because of him. It did take many years of making my own work to achieve some equanimity in this realm—this taking the mental leap that author and teacher Thaisa Frank calls "authorizing ourselves." It's a courageous act, and a teeth-chatteringly lonely one.

Unfortunately, even after you've taken possession of your own authority, the strangeness of people's reactions never really goes away.

Many years ago, I made the dreadful mistake of telling a cab driver, in response to his asking (en route to an interview at a television station), that I was a writer. May I plead here that I was young, excited, it was my first (and only) television interview, and my then-boyfriend (now husband) rode beside me in the cab. I could have bitten off my tongue within moments. The driver was Polish, and in a manic tirade began to detail the difficulties of transporting many members of his family from his native Poland to America. It seemed he felt certain that I could publicize (obtain help for) his problems. I felt like an impotent government official, and I felt very bad for the man. He was urgent and loud. And we were trapped there for the journey's duration, from inner city to distant suburb. My boyfriend murmured, as we scrambled out of the car after a forty-five-minute forced audience: "*Never* tell anyone you are a writer again."

To set all this dread on its ear for a moment, we might ask ourselves two things.

First, what exactly do we *want* to hear in response to telling someone we write? We might bear that answer in mind when responding to other writers' declarations. Warmth, curiosity, and frankness should make some inroads. I ask writers what forms they tend to work in, what they may currently be working on—*if* they feel they can talk at all about it, and even then only in a generalized sense: "a story," "an essay." Sometimes I ask whether they have any work in the world that I might look for. The wording for this is important. It means not *Are you somebody,* but rather the courteous *I'm interested in your work and will seek it out.*

Second: why bother telling people in the first place? Why not just lie, or omit? What's the point? A friend suggests that many do it by way of defensiveness, to dress up a homely self-image and hint at "fascinating hidden depths." *My day job, my family duties, my appearance, my economic struggle: these aren't me. What's me is this art.* There may be plenty of evidence for that. Nevertheless, I believe there's more to it. I think writers also offer the information as a powerful assertion. *People can think what they like. Life is short. This is my gift, and I'm using it.*

It's true that while the meat of the writing is done in isolation, external representations of the process can come to feel like a betrayal of its nature and its secrets. Worse, in the ripply funhouse mirror of other people's gazes, all our old ghoulish doubts may again flood forward. *Who am I kidding? Do I have a sufficient body of work? Is it of sufficient quality to count, even if my name's unknown? Me, and how many thousands of others?* That diabolical radio station that Anne Lamott describes, whose call letters are obscene—the station that damns and dooms us—turns up its volume, scolding on and on.

So it follows that part of quietly making a stand, in response to the inevitable, heartwreckingly innocent *what do you do?*—is a way of talking over that radio station, turning its volume down: pulling function into form. Words spark belief; belief sparks meaning. Meaning gives us reason to live. You write to save your own life. Hyperbolic? Maybe. But ask any writer whether that conviction is not her bottom line.

It's not only a product you're describing, or a brand name. It's a way of being in the world, a relationship to the world. To reprise Thaisa Frank, "Being a writer simply means that you have a passion for writing bound up with the way you think, feel, and live, and that you find ways—even if serendipitous, mad, or chaotic—to honor that passion."

To whom can you speak honestly of your work, then?

In classrooms, to the genuinely interested. To the young, who believe without irony. To fellow writers with whom you enjoy an honest exchange. To those earnest souls who ask at readings and really want to know. And perhaps to the handful of those closest to you, whom you trust to understand your calling. For a calling it is.

But pick your moments. And be prepared to change the subject—or to flee.

Never Enough

1.

There is never enough. There is always just barely enough.

2.

Both conditions have always felt true.

3.

I began working at age sixteen, a summer job as a salesclerk: a women's dress shop in a sleepy shopping center in Roseville, California.

4.

I wandered around smelling the chemical odor of new fabric, telling women of all ages and shapes that whatever they tried on looked terrific. Being there felt like being underwater, not precisely unpleasant. I found I could dream while folding, rehanging, murmuring. Time moved slowly. I remember the pale stillness of the surrounding day, eating my apple outside at lunch hour, the blank sky.

5.

I have worked similar jobs ever since, scraping together enough to eat, pay rent, take an occasional small trip.

6.

I worked during the years I went to college: babysitting, house-cleaning, washing beakers, canning peaches. My father, a college teacher whose pay was adequate but modest, and whom I loved desperately, would pitch in a few dollars sometimes. He'd sneak the money to me, stuffing a folded bill into my palm when I passed him in the hallway during visits home, because my step-mother hated me and watched my father hard for any signs of indulging or spoiling me, of which she could later accuse him.

7.

My father drank heavily.

8.

As for so many of my generation, especially its women, the getting of money, the infinite discussions, obsession, stealth, and frenzy around the getting of money, bored me when I was young.

9.

I did not, in early years, experience my scabby financial reality as unfair. I felt free, unencumbered. I never feared work, always found work, and completely trusted my sense that there would always be just enough money to survive. It seemed a birthright—an anointing. It felt endorsed by everyone admirable. Jesus. Lincoln. Yogananda. Hesse.

10.

I disdained wealth, distrusted wealthy people. They seemed to prove my private theory: big money—though it gets things done—

really, really fucks you up. Wealthy people wore a manner: the gleam of distaste in the eye, the lean-meat-and-white-wine body. I found them pitiful. I *felt sorry* for all they did not comprehend, for all the life they were missing.

11.

I traveled, worked, joined Peace Corps, lived in Hawaii with bunches of like-minded friends, moved to San Francisco, began to write. Always I worked, living from paycheck to paycheck with no second thought, until around my forties.

12.

Then the room began to shrink. Or rather, invert.

13.

The change felt sudden. Yet in retrospect, it couldn't have been.

14.

Slowly—and then faster and faster—it became clear: whether or not you were cute, if you had money you could go on living in safety and comfort and freedom and privacy, entertained and educated by methods of your choosing.

15.

Or you could fall down a sewer drain and die. The country did not care. No one did.

16.

Thus, attractiveness changed definitions. As with so much else that evanesces with age, moneylessness lost its romantic charm. The misted garland evaporated. In its place hung a smelly albatross.

17.

For men, the shift was deadly. No more summers of love. No free-spirited coupling. No longer could the Pied Piper, Peter Pan, or the Poetry Man get women. (In the insulated world of the academy they could, and still do. Outside that world, best of luck.) Men now needed a career strategy, a decent car, a savings account—better yet, an excellent line of credit. Prospects.

18.
A loaded set of parents could not hurt, either.

19.
My parents died young.

20.
When friends inherit money I feel jealous, bereft—and ashamed of that.

21.
Likewise, during a certain period of recent national history, when friends reported making terrific money from buying old homes, fixing them up, and reselling them, I think my husband and I both sensed that we'd missed a shrewd boat of some kind. We had missed our shot at triumphing over the game, even though that procedure, called "flipping," was bitterly uninteresting to us—and at some more troubling level, vulgar. Like a pyramid scheme.

22.
And it emblemizes, in miniature, the entire long history of ambition: of amassing wealth mainly for the amassing's sake—which in turn, naturally, was never only about amassing. First it was about survival; then about being king. Latterly, it is about winning.

23.
My husband is angry about money much of the time, for a million reasons.

24.
If women feel done in by judgments about youth and beauty, he says, measuring men in terms of wealth sucks every bit as badly.

25.

But that is the way it has always been, he says.

26.

He says that part very sadly.

27.

He also hates the smug, greedy, paranoid insularity of the rich. He hates the passing of the wealth torch inside families, and wishes everyone had to start making their ways, their fortunes, pretty much from scratch.

28.

I love him for this.

29.

Human suffering hurts him, the way it did my own father. I love him for that, too.

30.

But he notices—in anger—that no one in America wants to sit down and sift through the complexities of economic discussion. My own mind goes oozy and sleepy when he commences to lecture about tranches and derivatives.

31.

I'm not proud of that.

32.

On the other hand, the concept of *forgiving a debt* fascinates me. Like a magic wand, it re-rigs the agreed-upon reality—just because someone says so.

33.

Simone de Beauvoir said, of relations between the sexes: "Women forgive men a debt they didn't know they owed."

34.

Both my husband and I are damaged, probably, in relationship to money.

35.

He comes from postwar, northern England, where his family had no indoor toilet until he was a teenager. Newspaper served as toilet paper. Streets were gaslit. His people ate bread spread with lard; seldom saw a fresh fruit or vegetable. I tease him that if he'd been fed properly he'd probably be twice his adult height, and I am genuinely surprised he never got rickets, polio, or scurvy.

36.

Polio actually did quarantine his town once.

37.

He came to the United States on a Fulbright, age twenty-six. He teaches college. His father is dead, his mother frail and elderly. He earns what might be considered reasonable money now, while almost nobody else does, as the economy implodes. And in the midst of needy friends and relatives all around us, my husband often feels like the sun that holds a small galaxy in place.

38.

My husband also says that if it were not for him, I'd starve to death.

39.

That is close to accurate.

40.

Without him, I would be renting a room somewhere, living on almost nothing until I died.

41.

I would probably be shoplifting food. Not pretty, but what would the alternative be?

42.

He calls me Shtetl Girl because I am reluctant to spend money on anything but books, food, shampoo, coffee, and gasoline. My reflex is to save all I can against some dimly-imagined but imminent catastrophe. He teases me that if possible I would travel with a chicken sewn into the lining of my coat.

43.

My late best friend died of breast cancer at the age of 51. A divorcée, she lived alone until her death in a tiny one-room cottage, a granny unit in the suburb of a city two hours from me, the city where we both went to high school together.

44.

She was a gifted but self-effacing thinker and writer. She had taught college English, but to hold onto a health plan and life insurance policy, worked for the rest of her life as an administrative assistant, as I have.

45.

Admins, as everyone knows, are paid badly. My husband earns as much in an hour as I would make in two days.

46.

Like me, my friend eked barely enough from her job. Yet she scrimped to send a small amount every month to her daughter, who lived with her father out of state. My friend and I corresponded constantly, by every possible means.

47.

"I wish," Deborah once wrote me, "that I had thought more about money, growing up."

48.

Like me, she had considered the subject boring, never given it attention, supposing that things would simply work out: a man would marry her and that would be that.

49.

A man did marry her. But when she finally had to leave him (to salvage what happiness she could for what remained of her brief life), the cost was penury.

50.

I never thought a man would marry me.

51.

But I never doubted there'd somehow, always, be enough—if just barely.

52.

When I met the man who is now my husband, I did not suppose we would marry. Yet gradually, I became aware that while I was with him, there would always be enough.

53.

That was novel. That was new.

54.

He has joked with me that this is the only reason I have stayed with him. I try to dispel the notion. There is tension under the joke.

55.

Everything is about money, my husband says. Everything reduces, finally, to that. He says it with sadness. He says it, sometimes, with bitterness.

56.

When he says it, I can feel my mouth and brain seize up in socially-conditioned concert: *But that cannot be—*

57.

And then the words stop short of emerging because I sense he is right, that nothing has changed from the time we slew what we ate and dragged the bloody carcass back to the cave.

58.

More politely, I could suggest that little has changed since Jane Austen's day. *It is a truth universally acknowledged* . . .

59.

A wise man, older by a couple of decades than me, once told me: "Everything is *exactly* what you hold it to be."

60.

It seems the mind can acquire or discard a cosmology, like a pair of tinted glasses.

61.

When considering art, this fact can play tricks on us.

62.

At lowest ebb, I sometimes see every contemporary work of art—a play, a book, film, even paintings and sculpture—reduce before my eyes to a contract and a check.

63.

Or the lack of them.

64.

I can't speak for the visual arts. But a writer in our time, with lovely, enviable exception, pretty much pays to be published, in terms of the underwriting and spadework she must perform to enhance her work's visibility.

65.

It is one of the many quiet truths of making art in present culture.

66.

(Whining is very much frowned upon among artists, in present culture.)

67.

Still, I'd like to be able to put a pile of money into my husband's hands and say, "Here. Do whatever you want with it."

68.

"And by the way," I would add:

69.

"Thanks. For everything."

70.

That would have to stand in for a great deal.

71.

I used to fight bitterly with my husband about the fact that one does not make art for money. You just can't bear money in mind. (We'll leave screenwriters out of this.)

72.

But some literary novelists do, eventually, get paid for their work.

73.

And I have long fantasized that the writers who are recognized within our literary circuit, who have developed what circuit dwellers call Names, have all the money they need.

74.

I know this is a fantasy because a novelist friend, whom I supposed enjoyed ideal success, told me that her husband—a visual artist—once implored her: "Why can't you write a best seller?"

75.

I still assume that most established writers own a goodly amount of money, which buys, in addition to material security, writing time.

76.

But then, to make art and have money at the same time also seems oxymoronic, unless you are someone like Wayne Thiebaud.

77.

And even with the biggest guns, you never know! (No offense, Mr. T.! Love your work!)

78.

Any number of artists chafe themselves bloody about money.

79.

Read Scott Fitzgerald's letters. He was making what was then considered fabulous money, but ran through it fast and fretted constantly, crazily, about getting more.

80.

Most of us don't operate in Fitzgerald's bandwidth, however.

81.

Until quite recently, at lunch hour during the day job, I settled into the backseat of my car with a book, or with a sheaf of my own pages to edit.

82.

During that hour, I listened to the passing quality of the day.

83.

I've always supposed there were two kinds of passing time: paid and unpaid.

84.

All my life, I have felt that the only practical way to handle the insoluble riddle of money was to make art while being paid for a grunt job. Then panic would not seep into the words on the page.

85.

Also, you can use your own uniquely twisted little life for material.

86.

But the artist who has money, I imagined, would never have to entertain the above-named distinction, in the experiencing of time.

87.

But besides being patronized by the Medicis, or by someone like that rich socialite who supported Peter Tchaikovsky, how often has the moneyed artist truly been a reality?

88.

So why, you may reasonably wonder, did I squander precious life and time upon the day job all those years, when my husband earns a reasonable amount of money?

89.

The answer: he makes reasonable money, but not the equivalent of two reasonable incomes. I never wanted to become the wife who receives an allowance, who must wheedle for extras. (Not that I would have to wheedle: it is the psychology of being in a begging position I have dreaded with all my heart.)

90.

My husband has understood this. He respects it—if, technically, I have nonetheless been an all-but-in-name beggar.

91.

But he was always confounded, justifiably, by the cost of the money I earned.

92.

The cost has been deep fatigue and no little cynicism about the private sector's habits.

93.

In short: business eats its young.

94.

I was determined to work at least a few more years, perhaps buy a better car, before defaulting to a miniscule Social Security payment (if Social Security still exists by then) and my husband's generosity.

95.

While I worked I could afford to buy my own books, as each came out. I could pay the myriad costs of supporting my work.

96.

This comforted me powerfully.

97.

While I worked I could purchase my own plane tickets. Contribute to fixing the toilet. Surprise my husband with a pizza. Buy Christmas gifts, stamps, face cream.

98.

Face cream is astoundingly expensive. Even the lowest-level brands. I'm not talking about Nora Ephron's league.

99.

The late, marvelous Ann Richards, Governor of Texas, lectured women wherever she went: *Find the money yourself.* "You should never depend on another human being for your income. Financial security is the greatest security there is."

100.

But earlier in her career, addressing the Democratic Convention in 1988, Richards also said: "We believe that America is still a country where there is more to life than just a constant struggle for money."

101.

Hold that in the mouth and mind a moment: *more . . . than just a constant struggle for money.*

102.

Another writing friend suggests that without the carrot-on-a-stick of money, no one would do anything. Nothing would get done.

103.

But sex would get done. And birth, and rearing the young, somehow. And eating, somehow. Art, never least. And death.

104.

An "economy of care" never really took off, did it?

105.

When I chose to take an MFA in fiction through a low-residency program, I had to obtain a student loan for about fourteen thousand dollars. It took me ten years to pay off.

106.

My first week on campus I kept buttonholing people, asking how they were managing to pay the tuition which, to me at that time, represented a fortune.

107.

It was a source of intrigue to me. A mystification.

108.

One said her grandmother wanted her to have the money. Some, like me, stood in long lines to complete paperwork for loans. Many came from wealth—as simple as that. I would walk away, trying to digest the starkness of the disparity:

109.

You had it.

110.
Or you did not.

111.
A word about those Haves: They, too, have problems, only ratcheted up to a different level.

112.
Like why the second, massively leveraged, fixer-upper house has not yet sold. How to meet your nine-thousand-dollar monthly nut. Dodging taxes. Or whether people are being nice to you because of who you are, or because of what you possess.

113.
These are real-life examples.

114.
"What does anything *mean*," a wealthy man pleaded with me by phone long distance, late one night. Drink slurred his words.

115.
"I'm not a man," the same man told me on a different occasion, weeping. "I'm the moon."

116.
Back on earth, problems remain more prosaic. My day job laid me off not long ago.

117.
At first, all I could feel was relief.

118.
I would no longer be responsible for—and judged by—performance of endless, sludge-raking chores. I could let the files rot, vanquish for all time the numbing office banter.

119.

Then anger set in. Bad craziness.

120.

I felt shoved off a lifeboat. Assassinated. What good had years of *being good* accomplished?

121.

Never mind that it was a piddling, flunkie day job. Sleep fled. Burning-eyed, I stalked around filled with fury, then listlessness.

122.

"A real joy to live with," is how my husband describes it.

123.

Many applications of diverse forms of psychic first aid later, I stood on a beach and came to an understanding.

124.

There are plenty of ways to state this understanding. Larry Darrell in *The Razor's Edge* voices one instance.

125.

My husband puts it this way: "When you're dead, you're dead a long time."

126.

I've received some unemployment insurance. I'm doing freelance teaching and editing. And I am able to savor hours alone in the writing studio, listening to the morning air.

127.

How does morning air sound?

128.

Baby-sweet. Cool, clear. Pure. Still. And most brilliantly, *unattended.* Like a seabed when the tide's gone out.

129.

Is it worth not being able to pay for stuff?

130.

I'd be lying to you if I did not admit I still grapple with the answer.

131.

In the end, of course—

132.

When you're dead, you're dead a long time.

133.

Recently I was invited east to read to the university press that published my last story collection, and to the creative writing department that gave it a prize. Then I was invited to speak to a literary group in Florida.

134.

During both visits, I was wined and dined. Roomfuls of people listened carefully to my every word. They asked respectful questions.

135.

In Florida, I was returned to the airport in a chauffeur-driven town car. I looked out the window at passing countryside and marveled: *my writing got me this.*

136.

Please understand I am under no illusions. No law ever stipulated art should fetch anything, including a thrown tomato.

137.

But some sea-change is working within me.

138.

I am unspeakably thankful.

139.

A little nervous, too.

140.

Now: roll back the odometer to the great leveler, the great room-clearer, when the vain, pampered, blinkered American visits Africa or India or Mexico (or Haiti or Chile) or just about anyplace that is not North America or Western Europe, and with no preliminaries her face is shoved into humbling mud.

141.

Memory: the skeletal young woman nursing an emaciated infant, her hand outstretched for coins, near the Aya Sofia in Istanbul.

142.

More distant memory: asking my late father what struck him most forcefully about life on earth. (How I managed to shape a question like that during my ego-blinded youth, I cannot fathom.)

143.

His dear face took on that embattled inwardness—an expression he often assumed when he watched the nightly news—and he waited a beat before answering.

144.

"The disparity between standards of living for human beings," he said.

145.

It happened that much of my latter adult life, I worked for millionaires.

146.

It wasn't lucrative, alas.

147.

What they have in common—no surprise—is a flinty awareness of the bottom line.

148.

They can make things happen. They can purchase the best of everything.

149.

But they always, always know the price.

150.

They groom and cosset their wealth with meticulous care. Of course, cliché has it that that is how they got rich in the first place.

151.

But they carry with them a strange, latent anger about money.

152.

They feel targeted, victimized, unfairly taxed, unfairly charged, unfairly asked to contribute to causes that should not, they believe, be their responsibility.

153.

They watch the system, and use every method available to amass more.

154.

And here is the part that slays me:

155.

For them, I have seen, there seems to be never, ever enough.

156.

Is it possible for anyone to be at peace with the money he has? Or with that money's impermanence?

157.

Anyone, that is, who's not a Buddhist monk?

158.

After all, the money is only a matter of numbers.

159.

Numbers.

160.

The way the Red Queen's henchmen were nothing but a pack of cards.

161.

But they are numbers that can change the quality of lived life.

162.

Along which lines, I still grieve the conditions of my late friend's death.

163.

Though she chose those conditions, she paid for them.

164.

You could even argue she paid with a shortened life, by way of the stress she endured.

165.

Oh, money costs, money costs, money costs.

166.

Yet Ann Richards was no fool. We insist our lives mean more than numbers. There is evidence for this from the worst of times.

167.

There is evidence inside the toil of the daily—the uncertainty of the daily.

168.

Though if we're honest, it's difficult to deny that most lives, in their infinite, wondrous, wretched permutations, seem to wink out unnoticed, like phosphorescence.

169.

Irrespective of money. Irrespective of anything.

170.

But art does its best.

171.

Its raw, flaming, wild-hearted best.

172.

That strange flower, the sun, / is just what you say. / have it your way.

173.

Everything is exactly what you hold it to be.

When It Is Good

A thoughtful friend has suggested I cite some of the ways in which the calling of writing makes one happy—so as to ward off suppositions (logical enough) that the work brings constant misery.

One image comes immediately to mind, from a silly Tom Hanks movie called *Splash*. In it, Darryl Hannah plays a modern mermaid, whose fate is to own a pair of (drop-dead) female legs on land, but as soon as she's in water to manifest a glorious, scaly, powerfully–tail-finned bottom half. One scene I remember shows her filling a tub, two-legged, with the bathroom door locked. The next moment we see her blissfully reclined in that tub: a small respite from the bewildering demands of earthlings, her fabulous tail flicking once or twice in peace and contentment. The bath has clearly restored an ineffable, profoundly right state of things, straight down, if you will, to the DNA.

It feels like that to be sitting at the keyboard. Staring at black on white.

I'm pretty sure I was imprinted to respond this way by my late father—of whom I'll speak again later—a teacher who spent endless hours in the small den he'd built behind our Arizona home. There he'd installed air conditioning, floor-to-ceiling bookshelves, a first-rate sound system, and a big desk made from a wooden door placed on two low filing cabinets. He burned incense in a small brass Buddha, played jazz, classics, Broadway, and opera, and typed his head off—a rich, staccato music of its own, filled with the intensity of his thinking—at a Royal Portable typewriter which later became my high school graduation gift. The objects, the tableau, the sounds and smells (oh, the smell of the books), his relationship to all of it—shaped me early, at what I'd have to call soul level. Anyone who'd known my father, and had lived to see my studio out behind our house today—its outsized old wooden desk, shelves of books, Glen Gould on the CD player—would be entitled to laugh, because it would appear I'd done my best to duplicate my father's retreat in every detail. Most significantly, to assume "the position"—sitting at the desk, staring at hard copy or computer screen—is to feel much of the instinctive, deep comfort of the fetal curl.

Here are similar fits of gladness, gathered in a free-association search:

- Intervals at the desk when you don't know what's going to happen and it occurs to you, in the midst of it, that you're writing to find out. Your heart pounds.
- Finding a way through heinously painful passages that must nonetheless be told: being "accurately alive" to the framed experience, to borrow a fellow MFA student's long-ago words. Getting it right confers something and alleviates something, but I'm not going to use psychotherapeutic terms for these events, because they're different from psychotherapy.
- Rereading work you've made after a long time away from it, and feeling extreme relief to see that it still reads as it should.

- (Relatedly:) Feeling not ashamed but loyal toward prior work. It was necessary, it's still good, and you can stand by it.
- Driving alone in the car and suddenly understanding what the title must be. (Titles are such a strange and delicate business; one seeks them with a divining rod.)
- (Relatedly:) Swimming or walking or washing dishes or sweeping, and understanding, of a sudden, what needs to happen next.
- Going into a piece of work to clean it up, and in some bright flash seeing where portions of material can naturally fall away. The unnecessary words almost turn a lighter shade before your eyes. Grace.
- Getting up from the desk as if from a long sleep, with only the dimmest sense of how much time has passed.
- Being unwilling to stop, even to eat. It happens. (And I love food.)
- Bothering to turn on the light in the middle of the night to jot down the needed combination of words (or what you believe to be the needed combination) when it swirls through. Better to have the words jotted, even if they wind up getting dumped. Clarity comes with enough sleep. (Sometimes, out of laziness, one promises oneself to remember the words, stays awake for hours reciting them, and then forgets them by morning.)
- At select occasions when life appears to be hurtling on a high-speed express to hell, and in the face of absolutely no other options, you can begin to write about it. The act is private, costs no money, keeps you company, and gives validation, context, and some degree of control, beginning to organize the unthinkable: a precious, slim tether to the sanity you feared for.
- Images and words surfacing from memory as they're needed, from what surrounds you, from dreams that have the courtesy to sift through. A kid's name and face from grade school. Camellias in half-decay. A dead robin. An argument on a beach long ago, far away, reconstructed, transfigured. A phrase that pops into mind, fitting the need to hand like a little key.

- This may seem odd, but there's even a weird satisfaction in finding yourself stuck. It's happened before; it will happen again. In some bizarre way it's a signal you're *en route*. Somehow you dig out, or wander accidentally through a sideways passage, often unaware of the gentle solution until later. There's excitement in the trust you learn to place in that process, in making yourself receptive to it.
- Stumbling into reading that informs, or nourishes, what you're working on. Great joy, and the sense of a cosmic conspiracy—the good kind—wash through you.
- A note arrives from someone who was reached and moved by your work. That's the magic "message in a bottle," mysterious and welcome.
- (Relatedly:) The pure pleasure of writing someone whose work has reached and moved you, and (as frosting) receiving a warm response.

Many of the above may sound like the habits and consolations of a junkie, and while the comparison's somewhat violent, it may not be completely wrong. But the tradition (of requiring and depending on a writing life) of course emerges from a long, distinguished and not-so-distinguished past. Flaubert called it "a dog's life, but the only life worth living." Maugham noted that after a good day's work, quotidian life couldn't help striking him as "a bit flat and pale" by comparison. Entire books filled with such quips appear from time to time.

I recall a well-known satirical television program which ran, as one of its sketches, some film of a couple strolling happily through a city park while a voiceover declared quietly, "Neither of these two people has used any commercial product to make themselves more attractive to each other."

Therefore, if I may: none of the above-named pleasures has much to do with publishing.

Psychic Inroads, Scenic Routes, Culs-de-Sac

Writers' Networks, Writers' Lives

I've spent most of my life avoiding the companionship of writers. . . . The tribe is contentious, the breed dangerous.

— Pat Conroy

A friend embarking on a first novel and, in her words, "trying to be professional" was peppering me with questions.

How did I view the work of my writing friends and they mine? Did we read each other's work? Believe in it sight unseen? Interact on a regular basis? Was their professional company valuable to me? What about conferences? Writing groups?

I had no instant answers for these questions, and her prodding made me embarrassed for the lack my blankness implied: I seem to maintain very little formal writerly community; even less so informally. As I searched for words to shape a reply, I wondered whether this meant I had taken a wrong turn somewhere.

I suppose I think that most writers are a little crazy, in the main. That's not, please understand, to romanticize writers or single them out for pampering, but to state a case. Crazy is a kinder word, I think, than neurotic. It allows for colorful energy. It also allows for the inevitable strangeness, the outsiderness. If an artist's personal attributes don't fit well into the current social mosaic, well, *tant pis,* as the French shrug. Too bad. Most people have untidy obsessions and kinks and damage by the time they're grown, writers or not. My point is that there seems to be a fairly constant wish amongst us to build a kind of coherent, wholesome scaffolding around the essentially lonely, aberrant, and certainly unjustifiable act of writing.

I find this impulse poignant—surface evidence of a profound, and profoundly human, need. We're social animals and we like clubs, affiliations, and, for lack of a better term, cross-pollination. Perhaps *professional development* is that term, though I find the word *professional* troubling. (It suggests a shiny varnish of prestige, which strikes me as arbitrarily broad; maybe a hair silly.) Still, it's fascinating to see the resilience of our urge to connect, even within a group somewhat notorious for its irregular social skills.

So when my friend asks about networks, I feel a bit bereft. In reality I have had exactly two close writing friends (since I began this book, one died) who have sustained and consoled as well as edited and critiqued. I know many writers on a friendly passing basis, in capacities of student/teacher, student/student, mentor/apprentice, former-instructor-turned-casual-friend, acquaintance-from-parties, acquaintance-by-name-at-distance, and so on. We may kiss each other on the cheek at gatherings and inquire after each other's current projects. But I do not phone them or visit their homes, or e-mail them my longings or send them drafts. Those dubious honors belong to the precious one—*one,* at this writing—who (miraculously) loves me as I am, writing or no. For that reason I am able to seek her honest criticism, to hear and consider her ideas (as she will hear and consider mine) without taking personal offense. I know she won't chop my hands off. This is *never* an automatic given among writing friends, please, please take note. It is impossible to overemphasize that curious fact. It's a terribly touchy business. Many have learned it the hard way. Some artists go so far as to agree at a friendship's inception never to show each other their work. This may seem extreme, until you've been burned once or twice.

* * *

I once knew a retired man who had been a real contender in his youth, writing for *The New Yorker,* and, alongside that, screenplays for big money. (He was the father of a coworker at my then day job.) He'd also written a novel during his sparkling career, and this novel was, he confided to me at the time of our budding friendship, about to be rereleased. He pressed a copy on me one day, during a friendly lunch near my office. Of course I knew he expected my praise. It's likely he even relished the intervening weeks that followed our lunch, as he waited for my breathless call. Yet fond as I was of this witty, thoughtful, wry man (who, with a false modesty that broke my heart, spoke badly-accented French to the waitress at our lunch; then, lowering his eyes when I lifted a brow, admitted, "Yes, I'm fluent")—fond as I felt toward him, I couldn't force myself to crack the book. I put it aside, meaning to get to it. Finally I managed to pick it up at the end of a long work-day and read a few pages. And may heaven forgive me—more aptly, may heaven not perpetrate this upon me one day—I found it dated. Though the novel must have seemed clever in its era, its descriptions and characters read to me as musty, retro, and small; its smirking tone seemed an outmoded contrivance. I tried to enter it again once or twice and finally let the book languish on the pile beside my bed, among dozens of other titles I still meant to read.

About a month later the fellow phoned. He wanted to know whether I'd yet finished his novel-to-be-rereleased. (To my knowledge, this rerelease never happened.) For some reason—innocence, stupidity—I'd thought I could just let the book drift among its dusty mates forever. Never had I grasped (foolish, untried young woman) that I'd been *expected to respond*—warmly and emphatically at that. I suppose my silence was like ignoring a formal RSVP invitation, only in this case, far worse. Feeling the heat streak up my neck and face, I had to stammer into the phone to this man that my days had been so overwhelmed that alas, no, I had not yet been able to finish his book.

My older friend became enraged.

In a soft voice he began a long, impassioned damnation of me, a speech that gathered momentum like a river until it gave over to its final, bitter flourish: a curse upon my own work. Like the fabled witch who condemns the celebration which has not invited her, this man leveled his spear and pitched it dead center, dismissing my own writing as *women's magazine* fodder. In fact, at the time I was indeed publishing in women's slicks while I was publishing short stories in literary reviews: I was young and hungry and broke, writing anything I could purvey. His stab went deep. I'd been consigned to the frivolous and the shallow. It wasn't so much the danger of my believing in the power of his pronouncement as it was the absolute clarity of his intention to hurt, and to hurt in the worst way, that sank my heart.

I never heard from him again.

Anguished, I wrote him a letter insisting I'd never meant to hurt him, asking him to consider that he'd behaved unfairly. No answer ever came. I felt horrible, of course, stinging with the awareness of my blunder, saddened that his regard for me was forever poisoned. Eventually I had to let him, and the incident, drift to the far end of the queue of troubling events that we rework in our minds, worrying them to a cold sweat in the small, dark hours.

I was new to the game, you see. I hadn't yet understood the rules, or rather perhaps the *manners:* that if you wish to continue a friendship in the form you currently enjoy, you respond to friends' work with timely care. *Timely* means what it means. *Care* implies discretion. If you cannot read your friend's work in its entirety, you try to scan a portion of it to get some sense of it as a whole, and address that. If you spontaneously adore it, God bless America. Much more often, unfortunately, we are not electrified by a friend's or colleague's work. In these cases it's obviously best to proceed with tact; to respond with as general and positive a spin as you can manage without lying your face off.

Why?

Shouldn't artists, if anyone, be able to give and to hear honest, intelligent feedback from one another?

That would be bracing. That would be lovely. But despite what they may insist, people's relationships to their own work are as complex, idiosyncratic, and charged as sex. They may identify with it in ways no one can dream. If you prove yourself not to *get it* in the way they want, you may have shown them you don't merit their trust.

In other words, you learn to temper response to individual needs. With time we discover it is possible to encourage the *spirit* of someone's endeavors, and to address that spirit in thoughtful ways that spare everyone trauma.

A useful rule of thumb might be: *think before commenting.* You'll be living with the aftermath.

　　　■　　　■　　　■

Now, the more enduring kind of writing friendship is rare. It's something that seems to evolve over time, rather than march up to you. This is the bond with a friend who may or may not be a writer but usually understands your work's intention, who sees into it—sees what's missing, what's extraneous, what's alive, what's "off." (Isabelle Allende has consulted her mother all her life.) This nourishing rapport includes that friend's ability to level with you, without imposing her own rewrites. And this arrangement assumes *your* ability, as mentioned earlier, to hear her point-blank reactions without falling to pieces. Though you may feel disappointed, your faith in her is reinforced by her honesty, *even if you wind up choosing to override her ideas.* Her keen eye is reliable, fearless, and imaginative.

Oh, all right. Such a friend may be saintly, but she's not perfect. I suppose what I'm describing is a level of intimate trust with egos temporarily loosened, like belts.

My friend was the woman who asked me all those questions about writerly networks. Here is what I finally told her:

I cannot give a fail-safe answer about what constitutes a professional network, except that you finally define it yourself. The idea of a jolly, sanguine community of writers (or artists of any stripe for that matter) is, to me, wishful thinking. Writing is a solitary act. Yet perhaps for that very reason many writers can't help longing for community—for cross-ventilation, smoke signals, information, advice, gossip, much of which may boil down to *Is it this way for you, too? And how do you deal with it?* So they invent unions, associations, colonies, conferences, retreats, seminars, support groups, elaborate hierarchies of award systems. And of course they publish newsletters and magazines.

These latter can accomplish much. They run ads for fellowships, MFA programs, conferences, competitions. They also run ads from literary journals calling for submissions. Those journals are a good place for emerging writers to get started, and for more established writers to try out new material. Venues like *Poets & Writers* and the Association of Writers and Writing Programs' *Writer's Chronicle* are good sources of advice and updates, especially about the world of electronic rights and online publishing (what a friend calls "the Wild Wild West"). These venues also publish interviews with working writers, essays analyzing craft, and, most deliciously, writers' appreciations of other writers. They endorse readings that hone writers' skills, for craft and for pleasure. And they run letters from writers around the country discussing common concerns, from questions about simultaneous submissions to complaints about contest fees, to the ever-seductive, ever-maddening investigation, "whither a culture of letters in our century?"

I confess, however, to disliking a certain kind of writer's magazine: the brand whose cover often bears multiple shrill, come-hither headlines, offering step-by-step blueprints for every aspect of getting published. This sort of periodical likes to push its own dynasty of publications—now, inevitably, its own software databases. I've no doubt that the people who run it are sincere. I have made use of one or two of their directories, in trade paper form. It's my aesthetic distrust of those shrill come-ons that makes me want to run away. You can collect dozens of technique books. In the end, writing that has life in it can't issue from someone else's formula, like dance steps painted on a plastic mat. Anyone with an instinct for the shape and sound and movement of language must somewhere in her heart recognize this lonely truth, and agree to trust herself to go forward, absorbing the advice that fits along the way, tossing the rest. This process is lifelong.

As to inspiration, that's another matter. Many writers keep handy a little cluster of texts for consultation when the spirit sags. Annie Dillard's *The Writing Life* is a beauty, also her *Living by Fiction;* likewise Frank O'Connor's *The Lonely Voice.* Bonnie Friedman's *Writing Past Dark* explores familiar fears and dreams. An early favorite of mine, one that any aspiring writer should find (especially those just starting) is Brenda Ueland's *If You Want to Write.* The *Paris Review* series of interviews, *Writers at Work,* contains gems. Many writers simply return to their most beloved, talismanic readings—novels and novellas, short stories, poetry and plays—to recharge, and to remember why they're persisting at this strange game.

※　※　※

Some people swear by writing groups. Others loathe them. Those who love them insist they enforce deadlines, and that (if you trust and believe members' tastes and aesthetics) you get valuable feedback and editing help. I know women—interestingly, they are often women—who've spurred each other to finish novels by working through scheduled increments. They are pledged to this end, and they swear that this function alone supplies a writing group's best selling point. They also declare that since each of them is well-read and bright, each of their opinions "counts for" that of multitudes of readers.

Those who don't care for such groups (I'm among them) feel an instinctive need for privacy and for a pure, non-judging autonomy in which to work. They feel that input *en masse* (from even the best and brightest) can throw one off one's own scent, and that there comes a moment after the era of workshops when a writer must simply step forward and trust her own vision. Any idea of imposed goals and aesthetics, and even the general atmosphere of group endeavor (which can default to a kind of boosterism) leaves this camp cold.

To repeat: it may be interesting to compare styles and tasks, but it's *absolutely critical to remember that no single method of going about work is provably better than another.* Hemingway, as nearly everyone likes to point out now, often wrote standing up, often drunk. James Agee pushed a morass of clutter away from a small cleared space at the center of his desk and wrote very quickly, pencil to legal pad ("like shit from a goose," an admirer noted). Carson McCullers was almost never without her cigarettes and thermos of hot tea (laced with sherry). Mary McCarthy worked in any "nice peaceful place, with some good light." One woman writes from her bed on tablets in the morning when she is fresh, and transcribes it to computer later. Others write late at night, or in the wee hours before the family wakes up, or at coffee shops or in hotel rooms or libraries. Some do bits of everything by turns. It's amusing to compare habits, but trying to find a consistent thread snaking through them is a little like the old debate about the virtues of writing on paper by hand versus writing on keyboards. No one way represents a golden key. That process is yours to finesse over years, turning it every which way until you've got it closer to the way you like it.

■　　■　　■

Conferences and colonies allow you to meet people who may be able to connect you to opportunities down the road. In a best-case scenario you may meet someone you'll respect enough to want to extend the relationship. I feel I should caution the newcomer, however, that conferences and colonies can also have the backfiring effect of making you feel outside whatever circle seems to be the inner one. Names (with a capital N) tend to be an organizing principle of these functions. That is, several recognizable names tend to headline these events as selling points. They attract emerging writers who'd like to learn something from authors they admire. But such gatherings may sometimes seem to shake out into an awful rerun of high school groupings: the important, the less important, and the wretched invisible. This is not nice news for people who already feel like pariahs by being writers in the first place.

*   *   *

That said, the reverse case is as often the reality. Instructors and guest authors, editors and agents often make special efforts at writing conferences to be friendly and helpful to newcomers. They are eager (at least, they say they are) to encourage new writers and to look at new work. Many developing writers find huge relief in joining a dedicated group that is talking the talk and walking the walk. They make good contacts, new friends, learn helpful techniques, share enthusiasms, and go home galvanized.

Because the art is lonely, a Master of Fine Arts program in creative fiction or nonfiction can be a feast. It was for me. "You'll never get a closer reading," one instructor at the Warren Wilson MFA Program for Writers calmly declared at semester's outset. He was right. That program taught me to read widely, deeply, and very closely, in the study of craft. It gave me a superb list of works and writers to investigate in depth. It gave me instructors whose words had weight because they were themselves working writers. In workshops (though I dislike workshops) it mattered less what was on the table than how it was handled. I knew by then I didn't have to like everybody or their work, or be liked by them, to learn. Fellow students felt as passionate about literature as I did. Finally, the program enforced consecrated time to focus on these pursuits. I worked hard and felt invigorated and, to a pretty vital degree, validated. Some Warren Wilson students so love the patterns of reading, writing, and lecturing they internalize during their years there, they join an alumni group that continues those activities to this day. It took me ten years to pay off the loan I took out to finance my time there, and for me it was worth it. (But here I strongly encourage writers *not to go into too much debt for any MFA program*. The wildly gifted Anthony Doerr took his MFA at Bowling Green State, in Ohio.)

Artists' colonies offer similar luxuries. Each differs from the next, sometimes starkly. It's best to read their descriptions carefully and, if possible, contact people who've spent time there. Ask anything that concerns you, and ask for a frank opinion. What kinds of living arrangements are offered? Fees? Chores or services required? Co-colonists' dispositions? Atmosphere? Application procedures? Landscape? Weather? Food?

Colonies offer time and space. Sometimes they request residents to perform chores on a rotating basis, or to share a bathroom or kitchen. Sometimes they require fees for room and board, modest to expensive. Most are plainly appointed but comfortable; many are situated in remote areas to guarantee quiet and minimal distraction, and many in extremely beautiful settings. There is a women's colony in the Pacific Northwest which I am told offers a heavenly experience. Some well-known few are scattered along the Eastern seaboard, through New England and the Midwest. A directory now exists for these artists' communities, as they're called—from the Alliance of Artists Communities (www .artistcommunities.org). Their number seems to be growing, as does their determination to offer financial aid to those who might not otherwise be able to apply. (Some colonies invite or decline the applicant on the basis of assessment, by a rotating group of established artists, of sample work.)

Not everyone finds they can do productive work in a colony setting, though in planning for it, conditions may appear ideal. Sometimes people find they work better with the regular obstacles of life they've grown accustomed to at home, whether urban, suburban, or rural. Some find themselves unnerved by geographical remoteness, or by the sameness and simplicity of colony days: working in isolation, joining co-residents for dinner, plodding back to one's room or cabin for more isolated study. (Though many—particularly women, exhausted by multiple duties in the real world—find this sameness an unspeakable luxury.) Some are shaken by the seeming confidence of various co-residents, as if their work were flowing effortlessly for them. Others experience personality difficulties with co-residents—this, alas, is something no one can control. A natural sort of pressure bears on people sharing any sort of retreat, because the group is the only human social system for miles around (unless you have a car on the premises). If you want contact, your co-residents are it. If you find you don't much care for each other, even with interaction at a bare minimum, it can affect your mood at the place. But the wise remember they didn't go through the trouble and expense of arranging precious colony time for its social life.

§ § §

Please remember: there's no law stipulating you must like colonies, conferences, or MFA programs in order to become, Pinocchio-style, a "real" writer. Some experimentation pays off. Try things out. Talk to people. Collect opinions. *A calm distancing is helpful when participating in these events for the first time.* The temptation to feel sidelined, transparent, and unhip at various functions may be great. On the other hand, you may quickly grow intoxicated with the generosity of such coordinated focus and hate to leave. Prepare to resist hasty judgments. Make a deal with yourself about what you might reasonably expect from such a journey, what you plan to come home with even if it bombs, and what comparable experiences you can plot to provide perspective and contrast. Trying and discarding attitudes about the world of writing as you make your way through it is only to be expected, after all. We do it with the rest of life, don't we?

§ § §

You customize network efforts over the years. As a beginner who worked at an office day job full time, I decided I would use vacation time to attend one conference each summer, to remind myself what I was about and what I was seeking. In time that need fell away, but those events served me well during the years I sought them. Lately, I ask one or two people, at most, for response to drafts. My other writing friends—far-flung and known mostly in passing—I regard more as co-members of a wide fraternity who wish each other well but are not intimate. I might occasionally ask some of them for a blurb or recommendation letter. I would not presume to foist new work on them any more than I'd offer them my personal domestic problems. One obvious reason is not to impinge on anyone's time, which we all know is hopelessly steamrolled.

Writers can never ignore the perpetual, imbued irony: needing to be left alone so that we can make work which, fundamentally, strives to connect. And the constant paradox of a writer's will toward writerly community is that she must hold it at bay, much of the time, in order to belong.

For My Brothers
and Sisters in
the Rejection
Business

Rejection is democratic, and protean. It snarls straight out of the gate at the most innocent, and when we are young (at least, developmentally young), it can devastate us. I remember being told by a co-student during a break outside the first writing workshop I ever took: "You write like you're really, really afraid people won't think you're smart."

It was a sunny, sweet morning on a hill looking out to San Francisco Bay, a mist-framed dream of blues and greens. And in that moment, the delicate morning light turned toxic. I must have stared at this young woman—a cancer survivor, still bald from chemotherapy, who had no stake in polite falsity—as though she had just bitten the head off a kitten, because as her face read mine she added with quick alarm, "Of course, I think you are brilliant."

But it was too late. I stumbled out to the parking lot, drove home, closed all the windows, locked the door, and pulled the phone cord from its jack. Then I wept until I could weep no more. Was there no hope, no future for my gift?

It turned out, of course, that there was hope—but that a world of dogged attention and toil had to come first. And at every interval, in every form, plenty of rejection had to come right along with it. In fact, the rejection has never stopped.

I am rejection's long-term mistress, and I know all the old roué's tricks. I read the language of daily rejection with something like morbid glee: I can discern to precisely what degree a letter may be boilerplate, and to what degree even the slightest human intervention occurred.

Thank you for sending us ——————. I appreciate your giving us the opportunity to consider your work.

While your work is interesting and original, unfortunately I am not in a position to offer you representation / accept your work for publication at this time. Given my current commitments, I feel I would be unable to give your work the attention it deserves.

I wish you the best of luck in your publishing endeavors.

The above received human attention. That's pleasant. But its slippery escape, quicksilver through the fingers, seems to cancel hope. Notice, please, the deft shift of agency in the third sentence. *I am not in a position* to offer. Much is subtly implied. *Another* position might have empowered this person: alas, like a size 8 petite in the clothes racks, it wasn't, for some reason, available. The fastidious phrasing provides a kind of genteel American spin on the exquisite French decline *je regret,* whose rueful perfume suggests *it is out of my power, cherished madame, to affect this matter. My hands, only grant me the goodness to believe, are tied.* This is language that can actually make you sorry to have inadvertently brought about the predicament described, with its little bomb of distress falling upon the rejector. It is out of the rejector's hands and he regrets; oh, how he regrets. You want to console him: please don't worry. Yes, of course, dispose of the manuscript. Feeling better now?

Daily, I juggle the psychology of rejection. Since I choose to elicit response en masse, most responders will naturally say "no, thanks." So I play mental shell games to trick my self-esteem. I imagine myself the overtaxed editorial assistant who composed the rejection letter. Sometimes she's a grad student intern summering between Sorbonne semesters. Sometimes she is the hard-boiled, cigarette-and-Valium-popping owner of the agency. The rejector may be someone who's simply thankful to have a niche in publishing and an apartment in New York, even if both are the size of an ironing closet. Or she may be someone who's increasingly drained by the repetitive demands of her profession. I feel her fatigue, her worldly languor, her inability to be surprised by much anymore: certainly I feel her weary contempt-verging-on-despair, for the relentless cow-eyed efforts, still smelling faintly of hay, that land in her lap.

It's almost as if there were two continents whose citizens were at eternal odds, like Lilliput and Brobdingnag: the country of publishers and the country of writers. Infiltration of both lands by both populations is a charged, testy business. Spying, innuendo, secret deals, and official détentes abound. Grudges, vendettas, and favors are enacted. Emissaries are shuttled through secret passages. War and peace and war again.

Think of all the stories. Distinguished, admired writers who get NEAs and Guggenheims and Rome Prizes and honors upon honors telling of thirty, forty, seventy refusals by editors, agents, publishers. We've all chuckled over the quotes later cited from old rejection letters—I recall one that spurned Henry James. Inevitably, these notices are immaculately reasoned. Had we ourselves not been exposed to the now-famous product—work so entrenched that its present value strikes us as inarguable, natural as breathing—we, too, would likely be nodding: drowsy sycophants to these utterly sane and sensible declines.

Therefore, the determined writer shuts the door on all that.

Now we are in the war room. Here is where guerilla writers strategize. Maps cover walls, moveable tokens edge toward mock-targets on the table. Mailing lists, postal supplies, stacked and orderly. The coffee is fresh and strong, the music bracing. You start with good writing, breathe deeply, synchronize your piles, and start stuffing.

My game, these past many years, has been the direct mail campaign, including online and e-mail submissions. I believe in exposing the work to as many pairs of eyes as may be even remotely interested. In short, I believe in actively soliciting rejection—with an ear cocked for the small, dissenting voice that murmurs *I like this. If it's still available, I'll take it.*

These occur. They have occurred just often enough to have supplied me a body of work. It boils down to that, though it may not be a definition to brag about.

Then again, it may be. In 1999, a young woman named Margaret Edson won the Pulitzer Prize for her first play, about a brilliant scholar squaring off with terminal illness, called "Wit." Questioned by Jim Lehrer on the PBS news hour as to how she had gone about achieving this, the poised and cheerful Atlanta public school teacher told Lehrer she had mailed the script to every theater in the country.

All but one had rejected her outright.

This doesn't mean that anyone who saturates the nation attracts a Pulitzer, obviously, but the spirit of Edson's tactics should be required memorization for naysayers—and those who still secretly await discovery as an act perpetrated by someone else.

A wonderful essay by the late Seymour Krim in Phillip Lopate's timeless anthology, *The Art of the Personal Essay,* is called "For My Brothers and Sisters in the Failure Business." In it, Krim slyly suggests that the people who've in some way strayed from fixed roles in society have supplied its underacknowledged talent—the Jacks and Jills of many trades whose courage was of a special order. By titling the piece as he did, Krim showcases his subjects (himself included) in the light of their loopy, big-eyed yearning to excel at many vocations and paths. Ever since discovering Krim's piece I have liked the sound of its paraphrase, *the rejection business.* It evokes for me the vision of slipping a harness over difficulty and making it take me somewhere. Just calling rejection a business reverses its power to some degree. We can use this imagery for as long as it may even cosmetically persuade us: something like the "whistle a happy tune" effect.

The concept of a business also suggests energy: in this case, the peculiar energy modeled by Krim and his gallery, energy not daunted by official disapproval. This hardheaded drive is the psychological momentum a writer struggles to sustain. It means keeping up a kind of willed resilience, repeatedly shouldering past most everything we've been taught or internalized about authority, everything we've absorbed growing up about taking authoritative pronouncements to heart. Sometimes, authority is wrong. Or misguided. Or distracted. Or in a very bad mood because it had a fight with its lover. Or it has a stomachache, or an axe to grind. Practice helps us shrug off the sneer in an editor's letter. Practice helps us learn to turn away from cold refusals, stating again and again, "Fiddle-dee-dee."

Or its unprintable equivalent.

In the rejection business you stand for yourself, going only by some primal hunch—relying on weird odds that someone will eventually agree with you. This means doing, thinking, and saying whatever it takes to withstand the barrage of mail over the barrage of years, bearing so many variations of the same disappointing message.

Over the years I've received declines that were lofty and disdainful; others tight and wry; some icily contemptuous (signed, for a last, laconic cut, "Cordially"). I've been offered careful bargains: multi-page letters offering to *reconsider* a story (not accept, but reconsider) if I agreed to install the editors' extensive requested changes. (I have generally found myself unable to do this, but always thanked the editors for their time, and for suggestions which were at very least, I assured them, "logically conceived.") I've had two-sentence dismissals followed by the terse disclaimer that "perception is subjective." I've had one-sentence advisories that the editors would like to keep my story for another month to mull it longer, followed by the return of the piece with a canned note the size of a Band-Aid that closes with warmest best wishes "for placing it elsewhere." I've had notes summarizing a story's strengths and weaknesses, notes apologizing with encouragement. This last sort appears often enough to make my teeth grind: *Not this time, but try us again.*

So near, so far. You sigh. You go on.

In the lonely years of bidding for publication, the cycles of rejection and acceptance toughen us by helping us overcome the idea that judgment has a capital J—and this awareness is accomplished, like high school French instruction, by constant repetition. We are schooled by viewing, again and again, an astonishingly diverse range of responses from as many authoritative sources. This relentless feedback-of-many-colors teaches us to develop an internal compass, an eye and ear for which responses resonate; which may actually help. Most of all, rejection helps us earn and claim authority to decide without qualms what does *not* help, what fails to understand a work's intention or simply does not apply. Cultivating the ability to assess outsiders' ideas is a subtle, fine-tuned affair. Only you can sense whether an editor's suggestions prove useful; only you can decide how much to attend to them. No one wants a work written by committee.

In short, rejection reminds us over and over of the relativity of authority and the subjectivity of taste. Opinions from different quarters may clash amusingly—an odd form of entertainment that becomes a side product of rejection. I have had one editor write, "You do your piece a disservice with its last line," and another write, "Your last line takes my breath away." I've had agents and editors actively scold me for the insufficiencies of a story that *Kirkus* later called "a small masterpiece." (Please allow this, I beg you, as illustrative evidence, and not as bragging. *Kirkus* went on to dismiss my second novel in arch, chilly terms, and a writing friend consoled me quietly: "Welcome to the big club.")

One gifted author and former teacher of mine, early in her career, wrote a book of short fiction that her graduate school workshop-mates disliked, and they told her so. She was soon thereafter offered a contract for it by a respected publisher. So much for consensus.

What I lobby for (and will repeat here many times) is the slow-growth cultivation of a writer's own authority, through the steady eliciting and light-touch handling of *response*. Until you've established a personal network to usher you through—and who knows how much of that may still happen these days—submitting work remains, for me, a simple math proposition: harvest response en masse until that rare little note, e-mail, or phone call arrives. If you are struck by the resemblance of this process to that of playing a lottery, you're not the first to notice.

     ▮   ▮   ▮

Certainly, the game can make you nuts. You may believe yourself girded for it. And yet over years as rejection floods back in all its self-important language (polite, distant, vicious, courteous, dismayed), its redundancy becomes oddly funny, a taunting raspberry tootled at you every day from an invisible, parallel world. When the occasional acceptance does poke through, it may feel so alien as to make you wonder whether it's real.

Let me offer a couple of facts about that acceptance. It's certainly real. It's important. No one can take it away. You will feel like the Star of India for about seventy-two hours. You'll think, *Alright then. I'm okay. I'm better than okay. I wasn't dreaming. Somebody finally noticed. Now I'm on my way. Now things will really begin to happen.*

Then in best *Groundhog Day* style, you wake up the next morning facing the same big boulder at the bottom of the same steep hill. The phone does not ring. No one looks at you or speaks to you differently. The bills arrive and the refrigerator empties with stately regularity. It is as if nothing happened. If you're not at least vaguely prepared for this non-aftermath of publishing, it can undo you. A box of copies of the journal or book (that you yourself had to buy) arrives. An admiring note or e-mail trickles in. And then, nothing. Silence. All is as it was.

Nothing else to do but resume the ritual: reading, writing, and sending things out. Soliciting and harvesting rejection.

One thing has changed. You've added a line to your list of published work. That line will go into the next cover letter as you send out new work and bid for grants, residencies, and awards. It may or may not help get some attention.

Someone has postulated that there may be more writers than readers in America these days.

Which brings us to those sibling temptations: self-pity and discouragement.

It happens: an interval when you suddenly wonder why on earth you should not just . . . let . . . all the balls . . . drop.

Just let them drop. It's an interesting moment, something like trying to drown in a puddle. Because try as you may to sink into voluptuous sadness, it soon becomes clear you can't afford the time or energy. *Nothing will get done.* The impulse to return to work sneaks back almost independent of mind, like the propensity of certain soaps to float.

If self-pity truly threatens to blot out the sky—and heaven knows we've all faced these moments—put the question to yourself that levels all other questions:

What else would you honestly rather be doing?

If there's something besides the writing life you long to do, for Lord's sake, do it. *Vita brevis.* But if, in spite of all you know, you can't *not* do it—my sympathies. You're in The Life, and it will not likely end until you do.

During fallow or despondent periods it may ease you to go back to the books which fed you richly in the past, or to articles which sing of their authors' delight in studying craft. Charles Baxter has written about techniques of inflection in a way that communicates his joy in shaping ideas about his subject. The late Frederick Busch spoke in an interview about the challenge of persisting: "You're working in a world that is essentially hostile to the endeavor to which you've given your heart. But . . . you have to work at it as a job; you have to learn skills, acquire tools . . . [and] be brave."

If I go to the bone of it during intervals of exhaustion and discouragement, what I always find is this: *Your writing began as a bid for the nourishment of interiority, the autonomy and humanity of a life of literary inquiry. That was the first need.* Then you made your way into the realm of craft, and then, innocently enough (poor beast), into that of marketing. We lose perspective, as Thaisa Frank puts it, in a world of "endless social conventions and reliance on images." Marketing is still the incongruous, half-mad, cruel stepsibling of the work itself, the bizarre dues of the original choice for interiority. Each of us must carve out a relationship to this most taxing and fairly brutal process.

Marketing is part of what I tag, derisively in my own mind, "the trappings": the navigating and networking, politics, perks, rewards, cliques and gossip, the pitiless judgments and sour covetousness. These can seem to utterly contradict the purpose and substance of writing. Frederick Busch noted in the above-cited interview, "I believe there are certain writers who now employ press agents on a regular basis to get their names into gossip columns. That's new. I believe that there are certain editors who do the same. Perhaps it was always that way, but it seems to me to be thickening like an unpleasant smell. An awful cloud of self-aggrandizement hangs in the air." Awareness of these new trends and requisites can dismantle, even disfigure us. We may feel dismay at our own lost innocence: aware we've unwittingly crossed a line, been waylaid by jealousy and envy, perhaps acted badly—morphed into someone we might not like to know.

Yet to take the work seriously is to know it can't be complete until you've let it try itself against the chaotic field of modern letters. To write, for me at least, is to finally offer work into the world and take the attendant lumps.

Rejection, then, is like the wake of a boat: proof of motion. No action from the writer means no reaction from the world. To risk rejection is to risk reaction and, as such, a courageous step. Since reaction is the current that also carries acceptance, we can view marketing as a reaction-provoking tool. This does not mean being noisy or lurid—just talented, steadfast, and possibly numerous. The attitudinal task is to welcome rejection, at least formally, as

a by-product of reaction and thus a vital sign. It means, to paraphrase the old wisecrack about symptoms of intelligence, that
someone is home (your brain's engaged) and all the lights are on
(you're working).

When I have spoken with established writers, they have sometimes admitted missing the early, hungry years. It may be tempting to dismiss this claim as revisionist nostalgia. But as one famous award winner grumbled to me, after having attended his
umpteenth dinner with boring rich people who had given money
to some important literary cause and who'd thus bought his pres-
ence at their table: "I didn't become a writer to go to dinner with
these people." Awards and rewards are important. But many an
established writer speaks of the urgency of the writing as what she
or he still covets most, and in the midst of the successful book
tour what many long for the most is getting back to the desk.

Here then is the guerilla mentality in all its flexibility: that of
operating a reaction business. If handled with wit and determination, the lessons of rejection add up, gradually, to a strengthening
grip on the writer's identity: one who's staked territory, honed a
voice, created a body of work—one who eagerly attends the project
at hand.

The habit of art. A writing life.

At that point, neither acceptance nor rejection has the power
to paralyze. We won't be thrown so hard by the slammed door—or
by the one that suddenly, smoothly opens.

The Impenetrable
Phenomenon

When I was a little girl, my father would occasionally go on long trips whose purposes and particulars felt mysterious. They seemed to occur just beyond my view in a dimension yet unknown: a mountain's peak shrouded in mist. As a grown young woman I learned that the trips were often to places like Mexico City, usually with a male colleague, where my father was officially completing research and writing for a Master's degree, but where he was also finding as many opportunities as he could for what we would today call partying. My mother suffered without comment what she must have understood too well, and her mute grief filled the air of the home my little sister and I tore around in, heedless in our own pursuits of pleasure during the hot, clear Arizona days.

Yet it was those clouded images of my father's travels that came early to paint the concept of travel in my mind with a certain sheen—that of the unseen lands where he had been and his mysterious movements there: Things That Took Place in Shangri-La; things that must have struck the sparks of high mischief in my father's eyes when he returned, squatting before us on the front porch open-armed, gifts piled on either side of him. "Hiya," he whispered as we little girls heaved open the door. Surely the notion of travel also linked itself then in my wondering senses with my father's smells as we threw ourselves upon him: cigarettes, stale sweat, cola laced with bourbon, bitter coffee, exhaust fumes, spicy aftershaves—Aqua Velvet or Bay Rum.

In high school, impatient with the bland Northern California suburb my father had removed us to after our mother died, I remember taking a vow with my then best friend—a wild painter, whom drugs later claimed—that we would roam the world together; that in some year or other, no matter where we found ourselves, we would meet at, say, the front portals of Notre Dame Cathedral in Paris. Slowly I set about making good on the spirit of that pact. I started by walking to the Roseville Auction with that same friend, wandering amid the unhooked train cars along the tracks. I hitchhiked with her to San Francisco (blessedly and miraculously without incident) to wander Columbus Avenue in North Beach, keeping watch for a Kerouac clone who might swoop me up bridal-style and carry me off to the sea at sunset. It was the happiest ending I could devise.

Later I drove with other high school pals to Tijuana by way of Death Valley. I remember trying on a ring in a trinket booth and being told by the amused salesman I had too pudgy a finger—he pronounced a Spanish word for the equivalent of the Yiddish *zaftig*. As a young woman I had no second thought about hopping into the car with college mates, abandoning the paper I was writing about John Donne and heading for a Quicksilver Messenger Service concert at the old Fillmore Auditorium in San Francisco, two hours south on the highway. Eventually I flew to West Africa with the Peace Corps; later to Hawaii to live for many years; still later to Tahiti as a stowaway on a soccer team's charter plane; and finally to Europe several times, a child of the Occident walking the old, old earth.

These voyages sound round and definitive in recital. What confounds me now is memory's quick selectivity—how kindly it blots away the fears and discomforts, the anxious scanning amid the human pageant for my own destiny: I hoped to recognize it out there, I think, like a familiar relative waiting at an airport arrival gate. I hoped too, somehow, to sort my ideals, lay them out in distinct order—design a coherent life. There was a period in Hawaii when my then boyfriend and I kept our clothing in the tiny storage pocket behind the backseat of an old Volkswagen Beetle. We slept in a portable pup tent in a pasture shared with a grazing horse and washed in the restrooms of public beaches, gas stations, and coffee shops. In young years I never questioned these inconveniences, cheerfully pressing ahead toward a *clarity of location* (therefore identity, therefore destiny) that would ultimately, I was certain, reveal itself. Meantime I happily noted and recorded every impression—mailing them like a missionary from the field in letters to my father, who felt at least satisfied that I was mortally safe, amused by my romanticism, and perhaps by the sheer resilience of my will. I did not view the packing and carrying as anything other than packing and carrying. Journeying was the birthright of youth.

It's different now, of course. I'm older, and energy and time have assumed monstrous preciousness, so much so that for a short while I paid someone to clean the house once a month. For when I found myself scrubbing the bathtub during the twenty-four-hour reprieve from an office workweek, I scrubbed in fury, bitter against whatever fates had ensnared me in such a schedule, bitter perhaps at my own lack of foresight. (I'm back to cleaning it myself again. Those prices defeated even my exhaustion.) In any case, I've not been much inclined to travel. I've wanted to rest.

When in early years I read writers like Somerset Maugham and Henry James, I would imagine it possible (if I were clever enough? plucky enough?) to effect a life like those of their lucky protagonists. Like *The American*'s Christopher Newman or Larry Darrell of *The Razor's Edge* or even poor Isabel Archer in *Portrait of a Lady* (before she ruined everything by marrying so badly), characters who received the famous monthly stipend—dividends from clever investments or windfall inheritances which freed them to live independently. They could travel at leisure, inspect the world and their fellows at will. How this vision sang to me! It put me in mind of strolling—who *strolls* in America?—museums, parks, cafés, boulevards of the great cities. Time for reading and notation, for conversation without deadline. A thoughtful, unhurried review of the world. Sometimes that song still wafts like music in my inner ear. But its sound is fading, and I mark the change. I'm more familiar with the reality behind the scrim. When I travel now, it's against my will.

I am at first glad to leave the rutted track behind. In packing one always sees, like a hologram in the center of the room, that magazine-ad vision of how one will walk, talk, and appear to the people in one's path. As we select clothing and toilet articles and shoes, there drifts up, poignantly, that dream of ourselves in the scenes we imagine to come, scenes like advertising tableaux: we are handsome, knowledgeable, relaxed. Pre-enacting the voyage, we have all the certainty we could need: boarding the train or leaning against the ship's railing, wandering the city or driving the coast or taking some marvelous meal in detail-perfect surroundings. Ambience, lights, action! All in advance of setting foot outside our own door, we direct a little film of the dream trip and admire the unity of its theme. A getaway. Renewal. Soaking up urban glamour, sea air, history, art, rural charm, topographic majesty. And always, beckoning like the scent of a good meal, the intoxicating possibility of unplanned adventure, a spontaneous event or person, the chance of losing inhibition and structure.

All of it, of course, will transfuse the writing life.

What actually happens is harder to explain. Certainty proves scarce. Difficulty's the rule. Lines are long, transport delayed. Misunderstandings flourish, especially in foreign languages. Credit cards refuse to function. Weather balks, traffic thickens. Machines break down. Strikes abound. Illness or blisters or fatigue take hold after we have ingested different foods and kept odd hours with not enough real exercise or fresh air—or perhaps too much of those. Gone is the Ralph Lauren hologram. We glance around to see others looking equally haggard and sore, the same clammy skin, sweat-stained clothing, bulky luggage; we know they too have homes and routines and comforts they miss; they too question their present straits, unable to avoid the answer: *we chose this.* Here is the journey itself, transmittal of the body to the new location. Our clothes stink. We are packed absurdly close to strangers. Infants squall; the air is fetid with the stoicism of refugees. Secretly we rethink the entire proposition. What were we after, anyway? Oh, yes: to encounter, to attend. Perhaps also to sleep late and read. We were going to sightsee, walk and drive and view, argue about directions, eat too much rich food. Or take the riskier tours, hike to hidden ruins and get the rental car stuck in a gravel pile along a remote Turkish highland road, fear abduction by bandits, rape, murder. Yes. All these things.

Return means relief: gratitude for the known and—no question about it—stories to tell. Stories to write. These always sound brave and soulful in the telling; even the most frightful seems to manifest in Butch Cassidy sepia. Writing them, I feel the fondness afforded by containment: I feel safe from this distance.

But even having stories no longer compels me as it once did.

People vow that travel gives new ballast to the imagination. That it offers incomparable perspectives on culture, commerce, exotic systems. I would argue that this promised knowledge proves superficial at best. What happens instead, I would argue, is that we try ourselves—or the shape of the persona we would like to be—against an alien setting. That little more real exchange occurs with that setting than would between our Selves and a photographer's drop cloth. Dialogue is mainly internal, about our own suppositions (and how they may or may not have panned out). A different slant of light is seldom flattering, but it does jog introspection. For we are, in fact, then suspended temporarily between personae.

John Steinbeck is said to have noted, "A man puts his pants on in the morning to go *do* something." Most of us thrive in a routinized structure, a repeating principle or system, however simple or crude, to which we may contribute and which consistently needs us. Sightseeing, scrambling to pay for every next cup of coffee, navigating and negotiating—these gestures get old, become lonely. After a certain amount of time they generate for me the unmistakable sense that I am *waiting*—that we are all waiting, I and my fellow voyagers, for real life to begin.

As a young woman I never questioned the promise of travel. As a middle-aged writer I hold it at a wary distance. These days I most long to stand still, overcome by nothing stronger than my own reasoning. I want to eat simply and take air in privacy without haggling at every step. I want my own bed, my body ventilated and relaxed by enough sleep and exercise. I crave peace and order, having now experienced enough panic, crossed signals and spitting anger, races against minutes carrying horrible weight, indecipherable sound systems, contemptuous clerks, fumes of airports and buses, taxis and cafeterias, reeking toilets, mold and cold and humid heat and shin splints. I long to be still in time, not to move through it.

Right. I sound old.

＊　＊　＊

In one story of Edna O'Brien's, a protagonist takes herself to a Greek village to forget a married man, about whom she obsesses in lonely madness the whole journey. The uninitiated or romantic may at first envy the author's experience of the seductive pilgrimage she trots her character through. But with our own experience we come to understand that the Greek village, or any number of comparable settings, is an appropriation purchased, sometimes dearly, for the quick life of the "shoot": props and trappings against which characters and authors may brood or be distracted. (Also lacking in those sundrenched O'Brien stories are descriptions of Greek plumbing: used toilet tissue may not be flushed, but must be kept in an adjacent plastic container for a week or more until some poor unpaid member of the family owning the hotel carts it away for burning.) The other element of such ventures, so little raised in bookstore workshops and Sunday supplements, is the price tag. Unless we backpack like youngsters—as I did, as thousands still do—a good bit of savings must be ponied up by the middle-class voyager. Though I love Paris to my soul, like most, I can seldom afford it. Returning to face prosaic American routines and the dull boxes that pass for buildings is daunting enough; to face a flattened bank account is harder still.

How did my father see it? That travel was High Good, a matchless education. I know he was amused by my early wanderings: to friends studying medicine in Columbia, Missouri; to my uncle, a private school teacher in Colorado, by way of the Vista Dome train through the Rockies; to the summer job I worked at a Yosemite lodge; to the Peace Corps in Dakar, Senegal. But as he aged, my father also assigned more weight, reasonably enough, to planning and prudence. Though I know he was once intrigued by the Dharmic vision of the Beats hitting the road with a bottle and a song, he did not, as he entered his fifties, wish to copy them. He never found a good moment for travel in the years following his youthful Mexico jaunts. It amazes me now to realize this. He drove to San Francisco to marry my stepmother, and to Colorado to assist his brother through what, sadly, would be unsuccessful heart surgery. He flew with my stepmother once to New York, to view his old Brooklyn neighborhoods. And that was it. Though he was preparing just before his death to visit me in Hawaii during a pending sabbatical (the backseat of his car, I was told, was filled with brochures), he only seemed able to muster enough energy for the couple of hours' drive to Oakland Stadium, for a baseball game.

In a large sense I have followed my father's pattern. I went from exuberant, reckless gypsying to a frank wish for ease. I have become the thing I once most disdained in my elders: savoring the familiar; fearful of the hurtling chaos of the world, of crime and happenstance; taunted by morbidity. When I hear an ambulance siren these days, I am automatically afraid the disaster involves someone close to me.

I am sad for the loss—loss of belief in the possibility of an irreversible, rich, soul-changing osmosis between place and persona. I am sad too for the loss of the bouncing young woman, the self-ordained Margaret Mead who phoned her father breathlessly for a final goodbye from the airport on her way to a new life in the Hawaiian Islands. Wasn't that what bouncing young women did? I wore a long patchwork sundress and hiking boots, Botticelli hair cascading as I gushed into the phone of my love for him and my excitement at the journey before me. I would never see my father again. He died two years later, instantly, of a heart attack, age fifty-four—at a baseball game.

Later I would understand more: about his restiveness; about the death of our exhausted mother, who simply relinquished the will to endure his compulsive straying; about his haunted silence on that subject all his remaining life. For all I gained by my own travels (and as much as I would be able to mine them for my writing), I would never in my own mind be completely able to justify his—those early forays that seemed to culminate in the end of my mother. Yet some part of me, in a flush of guilt, senses what drove him.

It had to do with meaning. He was searching desperately, recklessly. As if liquor and sex were large, clumsy keys he kept fumbling with, trying to fit them into a stubborn lock.

For years—many years ago—I kept taped to my apartment wall a paragraph by the author Shirley Hazzard. It was from a *New York Times* travel piece, with lovely photographs. Hazzard lives part of each year in an old Roman village perched at cliff's edge on Italy's brilliant blue Bay of Naples. Most of her article described the village's history and layout. But the last paragraph, which I copied out and kept, was its surprise. It contained directions to that mysterious grail: the soul-making osmosis so many of us yearn for when we think of travel. Coming across Hazzard's paragraph again in my files, I discovered that at some level, despite all my practical weariness, I still believe her.

"One needs leisure; one needs imagination," Hazzard wrote. "And something more: vulnerability. Vulnerability to time interleaved; to experiences not accessible to our prompt classifications, and to the impenetrable phenomenon of place, which no one, to my knowledge, has ever explained."

Leisure. Imagination. High-ticket items resulting from enough time and enough rest; also, possibly, from a tony education. Money buys these—the kind of money, say, that bestows names upon its homes and estates. "Journey's End." "The Camellias." The rest of us must take a hasty, uncomfortable, surface tour.

Is it better than nothing?

My father, the humanities professor, never made it abroad. And suddenly I remember how I longed to have him beside me, watching the Acropolis recede as the interisland ferry sailed from Athens to Paros. Or watching the lapis-blue Bosphorus swirl beside a mosque-studded Istanbul, or the David reposing quietly in the Uffizi Gallery; or the *charivari* plane wreck that is Berlin; the little church in Auvers vibratingly rendered by Van Gogh; the wind-whipped arena at Arles; Rodin's voluptuous sculpture garden; the austere ceremony of the Louvre; the fairy-tale castle at Helsingor in Denmark, model for Hamlet's Elsinore. To have had my father peer with me at the grey testament of Dresden or the plaintive rooms of Anne Frank's attic, at the train station sign reading "Aranjuez," or out the concrete window atop Sacré Coeur—splendid Paris spread in all directions! A child of Russian-Jewish immigrants to New York City, graduated from an enthralling Columbia University, striking out to teach arts and letters in a raw, insular, distrustful Arizona—my father would have cherished those European vistas in ways I could never imagine, with his embattled comprehension of their contexts, of the best and basest things humans could do.

It was maybe just as well he knew me last in my vivid, untainted state, about to board the plane to Hawaii, joyfully on the brink. It is just this heady brink, I believe, this anticipation far outweighing any actuality, that defines us—that at least, for some golden while, carries us away.

The Vastness of
Geologic Time

Here's a non-secret: almost all writers of literary fiction feel hard done by at some point. Almost no one speaks of it publicly. It's understood to be bad form, bad energy. It stamps the complainer as a whiner: ungracious, entitlement-addled. Worse, writers live with the awareness that while they may harbor exactly the same anxieties as the complainer's, they fear his bad luck may infect them. They also reason, with a certain celerity, that the world of writing quickly teaches initiates its jungle laws: if you can't muster the oomph to assimilate, you probably deserve to perish—it'll spare you worse suffering later. Only the closest writing friends trust one another enough to let the true, gruesome litany pour out.

Nonetheless, the stories get around and we've all heard them: times when, if the writer spat on the ground, her spit couldn't have been guaranteed to land there.

Agents stonewall. Publishers renege or go bankrupt. Editors quit or die, or move to Costa Rica. Calls and e-mails—however carefully timed, however respectful—go unreturned. Fetching young *arrivistes* are rewarded; seasoned artists are ignored. Plagiarism, betrayal, dumbing-down proliferate. Editors who shepherd projects with an active hand seem to have vanished. Distinguished houses fall, or are swallowed by mega-conglomerates with Costco on their minds. No one has money: there is never any money. The more outlandish the story, the more accurate it probably is. The world of arts and letters only grows shriller, harsher, and more frantic as it shrinks. ("I'm melting!")

What words, however brilliant, will reverse this? Not much can shock us anymore, though we may feel briefly titillated.

Yet even the most successful writers eventually let it slip: that inmost, private beef, often about recognition in one form or another. This occurs all the way up to the Nobel level; artists may carry their anger a lifetime. (Doris Lessing was disgusted by the time the Nobel arrived at her door. Where were the award givers when she'd truly needed them?)

Sometimes complaint issues from a reversed scenario: writers become angered or depressed by the loneliness and vulgarity of success. Jonathan Franzen opened a long essay for the *New Yorker* (April 18, 2011) by describing his promotional tour of a celebrated novel as "without volition," noting he felt "more and more like the graphical lozenge on a media player's progress bar. Substantial swaths of my personal history were going dead from within, from my talking about them too often."

Complaint is a story, after all. A narrative with a beginning and middle, it ends with the teller's telling. No matter how cavalierly we cite *New Grub Street* (or *Darkness Visible*), no matter how rationally we understand it's all been felt before: when it happens to us, it feels new. And my sense, when I hear these stories (though I haven't yet had occasion to chat with Nobel Laureates), is that the complainer believes two things: his story is powerful, and someone, at least momentarily, will care.

I've been thinking hard in the last few years about the function of writerly complaint—and I mean now the sort that laments lack of recognition—partly because when complaint comes from others, I can't help making odious comparisons (*Too bad for him; pray that it never happens to me*). But I also think a lot about it because I've heard myself get stuck in it—enough, at times, to threaten to contaminate my life and work.

I began my writing life believing that no one could afford to waste time and energy complaining. It was like a choice to drink too much: always available, offering reliable, temporary relief—but by giving in to it you would squander time and (in the case of drink) wits. *Write or quit—but either way, shut up*, was my silent creed. Over years, however, the effort to market work has begun to make me sound more like those I've tried to avoid. Now I find myself in the creepy position of having less and less to say about my own path that sounds robustly good. This poses problems—for example, when I speak to writing classes or to smiling, expectant audiences at readings. More than once I have told aspiring writers (their shining faces, liquid eyes filled with dreams): "First, grow a skin so tough you can light matches to it." But above all, I fear for the vitality of my work. Bitterness in a writer is like necrosis. I've wondered how to scrape myself clean.

It's generally understood (silently, for the most part) that the frustrations of commerce and marketing form a special, separate chamber of loneliness for authors. This is far different from the generic solitude of making art, which most of us happily choose. The complainer's loneliness, during the trials of getting work seen and taken, feels imposed, arbitrary, and absurd in the extreme. She seeks witnesses, asking them, by implication, to confirm her perception: *Yes, you were wronged. No, that's not fair. God, this bodes badly. What on earth has happened to literary culture.* Some may view this as a comforting process. But if one's not careful it can overtake the rest.

Ironically—though the irony's sheer as nylon net at this point—I've had better publishing luck than many, even terrific by many standards: five books of fiction, received reasonably well before they dropped into the sea. The very first of them pulled a wonderful *New York Times* review. Each was published by a small press with tiny staffs and little money. Without funds to hire extra publicity, I tried every feasible way to promote the books myself. I've been invited to read at campuses and book festivals, received grants, fellowships, prizes, and awards. For all this I've felt deeply grateful, but call me a late learner. After over twenty years, the awareness has only begun to seep in, slow-drip style:

There may not be any breakthrough.

I had envisioned that breakthrough so clearly for so long, I could see the typefaces of the reviews.

One windfall would evoke the next. I'd quit the day job. A contract advance would pay off our mortgage and let us live on one income while I wrote the next book, which would in turn be received well enough to generate a contract for the next. Excellent reviews would issue for each new work, mortaring together each stepping stone to the next. Someone would offer a low-residency teaching slot.

I'd even braced for fan mail through my website.

Alas. Like Kingsley Amis's famous battleships struggling to reverse directions out at sea, I begin to understand that my progress will likely be lateral at best.

In recent years, my husband—a college English teacher—declared point-blank that he was fed up with the anguish my writing generates. He claimed the life had ground the joy from me and, by consequence, from him. What defense had I? Who wouldn't weary of a mate's nonstop woe, without even the consolation of money? Quibbling about the source of the woe (marketing, not writing) cannot alter the fact of it.

Thus—with my marriage atremble—arrived what my dearest friend calls the "come to Jesus" hour. I wandered around benumbed.

The writing's the thing, I brooded. Why can't it be that simple?

Because it's the Literary Ice Age, because the economy's imploded, and because we need to eat. We want love, shelter, food, and for our completed work to enter the world—and in due course for someone to notice and like it.

That sequence usually arrives to an artist with a couple of holes in it. Missing one element or another.

When, then, does it become reasonable to cry out?

We pick our moments. A much-respected author I wrote thanked me for my letter of praise, admitting it carried special weight because he had been "feeling discouraged lately." This is a gifted, acclaimed writer. He'd even appeared on *Oprah*. I could offer only a kind of helpless sympathy. That's when the ghostly lack of any single source of blame rears its big transparent head. One can say to the writer, "I'm sorry to hear that." But whom or what can one go on to condemn? Capitalism? Politics? Cultural blight? The end of the Greeks? Whatever *it* is, is never instantly definable: rather, it's more a blobby mass of accrued symptoms. Did I think less of the writer for admitting discouragement? In fact I felt relieved by his honesty. He honored me by not pretending—made me feel less insane, less lonely.

Then someone told me about a novelist now deceased, long admired and reasonably well-recognized in his lifetime. But during that lifetime came a period, apparently, when this man sensed he might not be able to sell another book. He wrestled, Jacob-like, with the question of whether to keep writing. "It took a long time," said my informer, "involving more than one sleepless night and glass of scotch." At last the novelist concluded that he had to keep writing. I respect the importance of his decision—if I also wonder what he meant to do with its products. We could say he kept his complaint quiet—except that my telling this story means he must have told it first, probably several times.

Not long thereafter, I spotted an article about a young man who'd played classical guitar since childhood. It was his life, his *raison d'être*, until the awful moment when he found himself playing for someone's wedding, or at a fancy restaurant: the moment when he grasped, as described above, that his progress would only be lateral. He decided to stop cold. Time passed, during which he avoided everything to do with music, as if it were "[an] old girlfriend out having a good time with someone else." Eventually he experienced a complicated revelation, during which he found that he could pull the guitar from the closet and play again—but *only* after he'd scoured himself of any expectation that the playing might lead somewhere. That, to me, ends what had been a superb parallel with the act of writing: one can't, in my own experience, just noodle for noodling's sake. (Some can. Godspeed to them.)

But the musician's comprehension—that he must revise his expectations—hints at the writer's task. Not to abandon ambition, but reconfigure it into something calmer, cannier.

How? A friend notes: "I like what the *I Ching* says about Innocence, by which it means 'not expecting, not projecting' . . . [a] matter of caring deeply about one's endeavors without attachment to the outcome. It's not about not caring about the outcome at all, is it?"

Look well. It's *not* about *not* caring. But *innocence* here seems to me a misnomer for *working mindfulness.*

This is where matters grow tricky. To be human is to desire. Buddhists and Zen practitioners and certain wise elders exempted—desire, for most purposes, is a vital sign. Do we wish Beethoven hadn't desired so powerfully?

Lately I find myself drifting toward the idea, like F. Scott Fitzgerald's much-cited measure of a good mind, that the artist's task seems to be to hold in mind all the furious, unrepentant, wild drive for the project to hand, *directly alongside* a placid, even peaceful, acceptance of (quoting a hand-lettered caption for a charming mineral display in the Arizona outback) *the vastness of geologic time.*

In other words, one must strive simultaneously with a steady awareness of the long-view absurdity of striving.

We've all met at least one or two artists who possess the steely equanimity that suggests they long ago cut a deal with themselves about exactly how crazy they would let outrageous fortune drive them. Their mouths may be set in a tight line, but they get on with it. (Choreographer Mark Morris has said, "It's just a review—it's not a gun.") Get back to work, these hardies advise by example.

Give it everything. That's where the joy lives. To what may follow, pay attention—but with compassion, wit, and (the lyrics fit here): "a clear understanding that this kind of thing can happen."

My husband and I put it back together, thank heaven. He has read these words and raised no objection. Certainly he's a marvel, and I owe him much. But that's a different story.

Dreams can be downsized, a thoughtful author once told me. And I'm still writing.

The More We Typed, the Better We Felt

Damn, damn, damn, damn.

I wrote a letter to the *New York Times*. And then, Lord help me, I sent it.

In the past I've managed enough self-control to write the thing, feel all the dirty satisfaction, then throw the letter away. This time I failed. All that remains is to hope they won't print it.

I try hard to shut up. Shut *up*, I remind myself. Be like those strong, silent icons you admired, your teachers during MFA days. Keep your peace. Chop wood, carry water. Get back to the work.

Oh, the temptation to vent is seductive and constant. Whereas the ideal, noble model, the Pure Artist's way, is to zip it. Silence, exile, and cunning.

It's a daily test. When someone reviews a book in such a way as to shock with his snotty cheek, his self-aggrandizement—I tell myself—sit on your hands and shut up. (Some other, better-known writer will upbraid the fiend for you under public gaze, and probably do it better.) When someone writes an article or essay that cries out, begging for your rejoinder—your uncannily fitting experience, your clear perceptions, your shapely, burnished language, alive with glittering wit—oh then above all, *do* shut up. Go for a walk or a run, or go to the gym. Refold all the clothes; arrange them neatly on their shelves. Then go to the desk, put your head down, and get back to work.

Otherwise, two things will become apparent, fast.

One, and most importantly, you lose juice through fulminating. All that thinking, all that writer vitality spent gathering and polishing language, all that ego fairy dust, gets rerouted away from the true work and down the slip-slidey path of opinion-lobbing (however justified your powerful feelings may be). Lots of rereading and gloating and tweaking goes on, not to mention time squandering, together with truly shameful amounts of fantasizing and speculation. (*Once they read this*—runs the thinking—*they'll be stunned by my laser intellect. Maybe someone will phone to tell me so. Maybe they'll offer me a book contract, a writing assignment, a teaching job, a turkey sandwich with Swiss cheese and avocado.*)

Two, your opinion does not matter.

Repeating that: Does. Not. Matter. Not until you win the Pulitzer, anyway, and maybe not even then. Your letter may or may not appear but probably won't, and if it does, the print version will almost certainly be serving as trash-bag or birdcage liner within hours. Worse, your letter may backfire, get you the wrong kind of attention, and shoot you in the foot. You'll be branded a crank, a blowhard. How good will that be for your work?

Silence, exile, and cunning. Why are they so difficult to practice?

Because writers are lonely. No matter that it's self-imposed: it's a shockingly lonely gig. No reassurances issue from anywhere, exempting a couple of generous friends. And because all our cherished perceptions inside this solitary life are held so fiercely close and given so little air and light, when they are occasionally allowed to stagger out they're sweaty and half-nuts from confinement. They can sound shrill, murderous, or at least murderously disproportionate. They may translate to others as ranting: dangerous at best, goofy at worst. Consider it. How much attention does anyone seriously pay to the Letters page, except for the sinful pleasure of recognizing names—and of laughing, despite oneself, at the terrible gravity of the aggrieved? (Terrible gravity can't help looking silly in most contexts.)

In fairness, the Letters section can also provide a moment deserving respect—that of witnessing other writers' boiling points. If an author we admire is moved to write a letter, we can bet she weighed the option of breaking silence and chose to do so because the occasion, for her, mattered that much. It's provocative information.

We might also acknowledge the bright golden haze of an arts-and-letters ideal glimmering over all this, talked up at conferences and by notable names, called the National Conversation, or Literary Discourse. It's a lovely notion, one into which I dive like a dolphin every time I turn to a favorite literary journal or write a book review. But in terms of the impact of individual letters—ad hoc responses to writing, or to actions or utterances by people notorious in these realms—though I may find them tasty as a form of gossip, in perusing them I seldom experience the reciprocity of conversation. Instead, only a sort of lame, mute nonconsequence floats in the letter's wake—when a second shoe should, by rights, be falling. It's the same sense of impotence comedian Robin Williams sends up in his British bobby's threat: "Stop—or I shall say 'stop' again!" Recall, if you can, the last time someone penned a blistering truth—so trenchant that by the closing "Sincerely" you were murmuring appreciation. Besides pleasing you for a moment, what effect did those words finally have? In minutes, the best of us are wondering what's for dinner. In any case, now that the internet furnishes blogs and social media to all comers, individuals who care are this minute typing madly away, posting details of their hotly-held habits and beliefs.

It's become a sort of babel tower, if you will.

Yet I wrote the damn letter, in a wish to prove something. I wrote it as easily as cutting pie, brushed the syntactical crumbs from it, and fired it off by e-mail, feeling—so briefly—righteous and smart, my heart pounding with momentousness as I pressed "Send." Whereupon my heart began pounding in a sicklier way: flooded with sender's remorse, suddenly aware of the dozen reasons why that letter should not have been sent.

I can offer but one defense.

Robert Bly once described the era of his youth when he and fellow poets were developing their work, critiquing one another, gaining chops and urgency—from his descriptions, a joyfully fertile time. These activities took place long before the existence of e-mail or websites. Never mind they could call each other on the phone or visit in person. They liked to type. Everyone pounded out their estimations at great, single-spaced length, on manual typewriters at all hours in all conditions—the whole passionate world of it, the meat and drink of it.

Back and forth flew the uncountable pages, analyses, discussions, debates.

"The more we typed, the better we felt," noted Bly.

A ridiculous *raison d'être* for anyone outside the game, but for many of us inside it, real as real can be. How much else in this world yields those kinds of returns so reliably?

Sadly, circumstances have changed since Bly's youth. Voices are many. Words, unfortunately, are cheap. Thus, for myself, the self-prompt must stand (wobbling a bit) for a great deal more: *Resist. Reroute. Write the book instead.*

The *Times* never ran my letter, I'm relieved to note.

But for a cherry-topping *deus ex machina:* as I finished writing this, I received an authors' magazine which featured—yes—a letter containing a quote by the late, indomitable P. G. Wodehouse: "Every author really wants to have letters printed in the papers. Unable to make the grade, he drops down a rung and writes novels."

What recourse, then?

Same as always.

Chop wood, carry water.

Revisiting Envy

I am Envy, begotten of a chimney-sweeper
and an oyster-wife. I cannot read and
therefore wish all books burned. I am
lean with seeing others eat. O, that there
would come a famine over all the world,
that all might die, and I live alone!
Then thou shoudst see how fat I'd be.
But must thou sit and I stand?
Come down, with a vengeance!

—Christopher Marlowe,
Doctor Faustus

How happy I am to be able to say it: I loved Frank McCourt.

(Hand placed over heart.) May his work endure and remain beloved.

I never knew him personally—wish I'd been so lucky. But I always admired the personal style McCourt presented, as much as I liked his work. Not only was his writing lovely, but (from my glimpses of his readings and interviews) so was his handling of his own serendipitous, epidemic fame. His reaction to it seemed just right: self-effacing, amused, gentle, and—well, frank. He lived, taught, and wrote a long time before *Angela's Ashes* caught the world's attention, and the consequent wildfire of acclaim never appeared to have even lightly toasted him.

To borrow the slang, McCourt already had a life; had one in place long before the media crowded around him. Everything about him, after fame arrived, seemed to declare, "My, isn't this pleasant—but don't imagine it's fooling me for one minute."

Now, if McCourt led a prior writing life like that of most working writers—that is, laboring in obscurity most of the time—he probably had moments during those years of envying the recognition someone else received. So his graceful accommodation of late celebrity struck me as the more remarkable. He had dodged, according to the late teacher and poet Donald Sheehan in an article called "To Be Free of Envy," a potentially nasty syndrome: "When the trauma of envy is repeated through the years of an artistic career—and especially when the years bring to the artist few, if any, signs of his own prestige—the effects of envy can come to constitute that phenomenon called the 'artistic personality.'" Sheehan quoted René Girard, whose book on Shakespeare, *A Theatre of Envy*, describes that personality, saying: "All people who live in the limelight . . . can shift quite easily from ecstatic self-adulation to abysmal self-contempt." Noted Sheehan: "Here, perhaps, is the most stunning fact about the long-range effects of such shifts: even if the artist finally, after long years of neglect, achieves spectacular levels of prestige, he will nevertheless continue to know himself only by means of these whip-saw effects of habituated envy."

And yet who among us, I wonder, has been immune to envy? Who has not felt the silent, hard internal pinch when someone we know or recognize is given the royal nod for advancement we seek—the story accepted, the grant bequeathed, the book sold, the warm blurb or review, the excerpt in the glossy venue, the important award? Without warning, a catch of wild woe squeezes somewhere below the breastbone, followed by a wormy sense of ineffectiveness—perhaps an electrical prickling of dread. *Oh, no,* we think. And who has not then instantly loathed, yet been held fast by, his own meanness?

To feel in those first seconds not the pleasure for the excellent writer that you assumed you would feel (and remind yourself you absolutely *should* feel), but rather a tiny, long, invisible needle piercing you clean through—to feel this is also to be flushed with two kinds of horror: One insidiously questions your own work. The other questions your fitness to be doing the art. Surely those who have themselves in hand don't think this way! Yet inside, a banshee howls. *How long?* cries the trapped madwoman. *How long before I get some help here?* Guilt adds to dismay. You may find yourself paralyzed, depressed, unable to work for a while.

There is a real quality of ambush to it.

At its peak, envy challenges us to a wrestle, silent and desperate, for the life of the writing spirit. To let that be harmed or contaminated seems the worst fate of all. So we ferociously block out self-pity, a luxury we can't afford. On special occasions, yes, it might be briefly permitted—a deliciously stupefying wallow, like drinking tequila while steeped in a hot bath. But use caution when wallowing: self-pity is also a notoriously greedy diverter of energy.

And energy, my friends, is the ballgame.

People cluck, "It's natural to feel envious." No help. (Lots of ghastly things are "natural.") Envy seems to enter the veins and travel the body like venom: weakening, debilitating. Compounding these effects is the awareness that by weighting various external symbols of reward, envy threatens to stunt or taint the integrity of the impulse to make art in the first place—to blight the wholeness and unfetteredness of the act. (One miserable man, according to Sheehan, told psychiatrist Robert Coles he would prefer to have been cursed with any other behavioral disorder, any other addiction, however terrible, than that of his predisposition to envy.)

I have long wished to dissect envy, in a naïve yearning to be rid of it. Writers like to peer at the forbidden, to tease out components of the monstrous; why not spotlight envy, turning it like mildew toward the noon sun to banish it? Heaven knows envy's democratic enough; old and young, published and unpublished do their time on one or the other end of the strained congratulatory remarks, the sharp reconfigurations of the face. A writing teacher I admire once mused to a class: "Writers are some of the least charitable people there are."

Must this be so?

Yes, claims a writing friend. Why? Because a writer's product is so immutably bound up with ego and exposed self (she declares) that it stands for the self in a way that surgery or accounting or gardening or even virtuoso musicianship—inspired techniques, fundamentally—don't quite parallel. What is more, my friend argues, it would not matter whether there was plenty of well-paid publishing space for all; because writing's result is pure, exposed self, we begrudge the external judgment, the triumph of one over another.

I believe, though, that numbers play a tremendous part. Competition for attention in the modern literary arena has exploded. Channels of influence are whimsical, to put it kindly; money's often absent or parsed in brave little cookie-sale bundles. Apparatus of commercial publishing and critical appraisal resemble the stock exchange, a shouting free-for-all. Publishers and agents, as John Baker of *Publisher's Weekly* once noted, have become "equivocal and migratory." Contracts are cancelled. Agents woo like new lovers, then disappear. Keeping equilibrium amidst all this, let alone dignity, is tough. Surely a huge reason for petulance among writers is that mainstream venues for their work are so weirdly, competitively few—ironically, because of an infotainment industry shifting into overdrive, in which superstores, book groups, websites, and Oprah boosterism proliferate as national pastimes, cutting off coexistence room for the quieter mid-list titles. For writers of literary fiction—whose work editors may so admire they pass it around the office for colleagues to enjoy before declaring it commercially unjustifiable—the whole business can feel like a vicious game of musical chairs.

At the same time, envy's an old, old reflex. Since before King David, people have coveted each other's power, money, belongings, beauty, spouses or lovers, talent, status, and, never least, health. But in present time, envy may be the last of the human foibles to which we easily confess. None of the writing friends I polled had a ready antidote for it other than a kind of vague, troubled fatalism. Most got depressed awhile. Some claimed they only envied when they felt the objects of their envy hadn't deserved their desserts.

"I think envy is a part of life, really," offered a wise friend, "not just limited to the arts, but certainly intensified there. When somebody gets something you are working very hard to get, then how can you not be envious? In such cases envy even seems a reasonable response. Iago, for heaven's sake, has some cause. Not that I recommend his course of action. We have a sense of fair play, and I think when that sense is violated, then we envy in proportion to that perceived violation—even though we all know life isn't fair."

Writers walk a tense tightwire between the drive to make work and the ambition also necessary to it. On the one hand we sense uncomfortably that it diminishes us to become too entangled with careerism, honors, and rewards. Too much attention to these seems to demean the work itself, reducing it by comparison to something flat and allusive, incidental—even throwaway, like Monopoly money. ("I had a story in *Best American*. Who are you?") In this climate, paranoia and anxiety for "positioning" spread like viruses. To harbor them risks infecting one's beliefs and dreams— those other essentials of the ballgame, propelled by that first necessity, energy.

On the other hand, to write is to be compelled to complete the gesture, which requires getting the work seen, taken, and marketed as effectively as possible. There floats among writers a tacit ethos that it is bad form to bring up this subject, and worse yet to cavil too long about it. The thing to do is shut up and keep working: all else, as one wry mentor puts it, is "barking and scratching." Yet each must find a way to live with her human fallibility, and with the ever-present irony: *the act of writing carries an intrinsic humanity that the politics of ambition always seems, by definition, to defile.*

＊　　＊　　＊

In her wonderful book of essays, *Writing Past Dark,* Bonnie Friedman calls envy "the writer's disease," characterizing it as an insatiable demon devouring itself. She quotes a medieval poem depicting envy as a lean, gnawed-away wraith, rocking obsessively in a dark corner. Friedman suggests, as did Donald Sheehan, that envy and vanity are two sides of the same self-sabotaging impulse. This demon stands well apart from the working self, pointing and mocking, always starving (no matter what good things have come) precisely because it stands apart from true engagement, feeding on the non-nourishment of popular measure, craving external awards and reassurances—craving these without cease and without satisfaction. Few among us are exempt: national and international laureates may nurse bitter resentments to their last breaths, which may baffle even their closest friends. Recognition too late? Wrong kind? Not enough? These anguishes may well stem from a lifetime's "whip-saw effects of habituated envy." (Again, this is why McCourt shines so brightly by comparison.)

To Donald Sheehan, envy was a spiritual ailment, and so he proposed a spiritual remedy. At each poetry conference he taught, he commanded his fifty or so participants: "You are here at this conference to make—not your own art—but the art of at least one other person here better and fuller and richer. You are here to fall so much in love with another person's poems that you would give all your art over to them—freely, deeply, unhesitatingly—so that these poems, and their poet, can become more beautifully and movingly true." Sheehan insisted that at every conference, for the most part, this injunction worked. "[A]s our envy diminishes, we often experience the arrival of what may well be our first real friendships since early childhood, friendships within which—and through which—our own art grows richer and fuller."

I recognize the genius of his advice: that to some extent, function must follow form; that grace comes with a reversal of energy, in turning from Self to minister to the Other. (It should be respectfully noted here that Sheehan also served as a subdeacon of the Holy Resurrection Orthodox church, in New Hampshire.)

Genuine admiration for other people's work is a real and happy occasion. But from my own experience, friendship, in or outside of writing circles, may or may not have much to do with a fair assessment of someone's work. Humility as a spiritual exercise may be good for us, and for making warm connections. But the mix of humility with necessary audacity in the struggle to "get it right" is a complex, individualized event. Certainly we have many modern writers who embody the generosity Sheehan admired, whose affection and rigor as teachers are legendary. But this ability, if inspiring, is neither given to all nor suited to all. Humility is surely better encountered than assigned. Falling in love, I sense, is a windfall.

▓   ▓   ▓

From time to time I have singled out a writer and idealized her, convincing myself she had everything: recognition, love, security, time. In my mind I would build a world around her and people it with brilliance. And sooner than later I'd learn some muddying fact: The marriage had fallen apart. There were dreadful money problems or health crises or lawsuits, family difficulties, even tragedies. I do not describe any one profile but a generalized experience, a theme repeated with innumerable individual variations over years. This, for me, teaches humility. Unless you are Gore Vidal, you never wanted bad things to happen to those you envied. (Vidal is said to have quipped, "It isn't enough that I succeed; my friends must fail.")

But while we live and work and have ambition, no one is cured of the writers' disease. Envy and jealousy still lash out in unguarded moments like a hidden nest of tiny snakes, and the poison commences its awful journey to the heart. To your own exasperation you may find yourself yet again wincing, slumping, uttering some caustic remark, pining for other writers' good fortune while perfectly aware you may not care to endure their lives' fine print. Instead you stubbornly envision those people's perfect conditions and want them: Their fat bank accounts. Their silent mornings. Their devoted, accommodating families and friends. Their underwritten travel and standing-room-only readings. All the refreshing sleep they have ever gotten and all they expect to get. The multiple-book contracts, loyal agents and publicists, many-thousands-of-copies print runs, paid teaching or lecture or residency fellowships, the respectful reviews, automatic entrée into colonies and retreats, guest appearances in the best journals and highbrow slicks.

And then?

If, for a change, we chose to lean into envy as far as imaginatively possible, all the way to the inevitable Faustian pact of agreeing to forfeit this existence for the existence we think we prefer—forfeiting memory of course, love and desire, trauma, joy, all the billion and one perceptions, dreams, and experiences *that shaped the sensibility we now claim as mind and voice*—then consider: Not only would we be agreeing to slip inside the skin of the Other and live out the rest of our life there. We would also be agreeing to erase the life that created our own writing. In some Möbius strip of confrontative logic, such a pact would mean annulling the conscious self. And perhaps that's finally the burden we most long to eliminate: the torment of our own consciousness. Erratic, anarchic consciousness, miserably prey to all manner of flattery and distraction, incomplete, shape-shifting—and utterly necessary to the making of art.

Like Bonnie Friedman, I sense that resistance to envy makes it like a Chinese finger-puzzle: its grasp only tightens. Perhaps the most workable tack is simply to dwell patiently with envy until it fades. As Paul Auster has more than once stated quietly of the craft, you do it because you have to. All writerly roads must lead to this: if you can live without writing, you should. If your work indeed has life and you persevere, response is likely, if not guaranteed, to occur. What can be harnessed from raw envy, perhaps, is a kind of sour jump-start. Residual emotion sends you back to the desk with resolve. Familiar rhythms take over and soothe (and lead you away from externals). This may also be an interval in which—patiently, gently, like counting fingers and toes—to re-think the enterprise: to recall that writing and reading are ways of keeping the habit of art, of interiority, of investigative invention.

At the very least we can practice defusing envy by inviting it in, mulling it over, and waiting politely with it until it gets bored and leaves. At the very least we can practice separating it from the working self: *Oh yes, right, you again. Well, hello. Let's see if I have any tea around here. Will orange juice do?*

Gumby, Frankenstein, Jakob, Rosamund

The word *character* abrades me, though there's never been a good alternative to it. For me the word's sound, read or spoken, reduces its image to something flat and cartoonish, Gumby-like and spatulate, a group of slouchy Popeyes or pup-faced goofs. *What a character. What a bunch of characters.* We shake our heads. This aura of caricature (that word again), which ultimately suggests puniness, aggravates me because I take character (and everything else about literary fiction) with desperate seriousness, and I seek the same urgency in the work of others, even when that work is meant to be funny.

So I rarely think of those humanoid entities I make, or encounter in literature, as *characters.* I don't reach for that word to describe them. Yet I can't feel right calling them *people.* I have no word for them. A strange preserving ether envelops them, separating them from all else. Though I've often felt irritated by authors who speak of their characters in the third person like fond old friends, I catch myself at it. Because (yes, reams have been written about this) characters can feel so real to both author and reader that we believe we own them, or rather, that we *own the accurate perception* of them—a big reason that films made of beloved books often appall us. ("Oh, no! They got her/him all wrong.") Characters are living dreams for both reader and writer—private, enduring holograms in the life of our days. Some are capable of a rich array of gestures, and we hold close everything about them.

In his book of essays on writing, *The Half-Known World,* novelist Robert Boswell argues for mining the deep lode of mystery inherent in character (rather than over-determining it by concocting personality profiles, genetic and genealogical histories, résumés, and the like) because of course it's the inconsistency that pops, the surprise that gives verisimilitude. ("No surprise for the writer, no surprise for the reader," declares Thaisa Frank.) Amen to this. But when he asks a series of questions calculated to flick authorial control off-balance—Why does your character believe she should be fired? What would your character tell you she thought of you, after a few drinks, in a bar?—the repeated words *your character* embarrass me, as if I am playing with paper dolls, making their arms go up and down. Even if this is technically true, I cannot bear letting the matter stand (or flop over) there. It's more, more. The whole enterprise of drawing individuals forth from experience and imagination feels like a treasure hunt in a dream—one so packed with portent, I lack language for it.

It's tempting to spy in the house of your own craft: to try to discern, and map, a consistent method of making character. But I sense danger there. In her enchanting essay collection, *A Plea for Eros,* novelist Siri Hustvedt writes of Henry James: "I think that James felt that every attempt to reduce life to a system of beliefs . . . must inevitably become a form of lying." If we substitute for *life* the words *craft* or *technique,* we may be onto something. Naturally, it's human (and pandemic) to try to shape a system of beliefs about nearly everything. It's a survival tactic, how we navigate a relationship to the daily. (Hustvedt also noted, in a different essay, "I am making . . . and not making [my characters], like people in my dreams.") I am not lobbying for voodoo or piety, nor denying the lifelong feast of studying craft, but am leery of any writing advice smacking of recipes. (Add one florid nose, an orange wig, a sneeze that sounds like a squeak, etc.) In the brilliant compendium *A William Maxwell Portrait,* Shirley Hazzard cites, in her essay, one of author Maxwell's best strengths (emphasis mine): "He had *the writer's need to defend the secret writing mind,* where objectivity and syllables must alike be nurtured and weighed, and the deeper, unshared self explored and plundered for treasure."

It is that secret mind I can never adequately explain nor myself fully understand, yet feel bound to protect, nourish, and defend. As I devoured James Woods's *How Fiction Works* (a series of appreciations so fine you want to restart the book the moment you finish), I noticed with relief that Woods does not prescribe for making character, but rather analyzes (in a state resembling exaltation) how any number of memorable characters manifest, noting more than once that writers teach readers how to read their works. Woods can intensify the magnification on the examining lens and identify with superb precision what elements make characters memorable—and to some degree, how that appears to have been done. But there's the rub: one cannot then run off and try to repeat a successful formula. The paradox of studying craft is that a writer must let what she observes seep in, or up, if you will, from the base of the brain—from a place not entirely conscious. There's never been a good way to justify or explain this.

Certainly, I'm guilty of the Frankenstein method. I knew someone, who knew someone. Both fed into a new Someone, who became their composite but more, and different. And I pray the reader won't notice the swollen purple incisions and black sutures where pieces of four women were sewn into the twenty-eight-year old editor called Alex (for my novel *Miss Kansas City*). She's none of those others but assembled with their body parts and packed with mixed portions of their stuffing, including an obsessive love affair with a famous, older, married man and a craving for the chocolate spread Nutella, devoured by the spoonful. I was certain I knew how she'd respond to almost anything—until the day she cracked out of excruciating shyness, maddened by her betraying lover's smugness, and (using a running start) shoved him off the dock into the icy, wind-chopped waters of Sausalito Harbor.

And yet I honestly hate it when authors talk that way.

It sounds chummy. Exclusionary. It also shrinks the fictional dream by suggesting that a character's real essence is locked into some secret pact between author and character—key data only released (like the flavored syrup at the center of a piece of chewing gum) during interviews with the author—when instead we know that each reader has built a detailed, internal vision of the story's world and all its denizens, every stitch of which feels, to that reader, unassailable. We "bustle about," notes Sven Birkerts (an image I love), constructing the story's dream.

A related confession: because literary characters I cherish are stored in a half-dream-state (with other stories that have entered me for life), I can't always remember their names or details. What grips, what haunts, what is obtainable in an instant, is the feeling they gave. (For that matter, do we not remember books themselves, when characters' names and even plots are long swallowed by memory's mists, for exactly that, the feeling they gave? Don't we recall entire periods of our lives this way?) I had to resort to the internet to locate the name Jakob Beer, that of the terrified boy in Anne Michaels's exquisite 1999 novel, *Fugitive Pieces.* Jakob grows into a tenderly complex poet, thanks to his rescue by geologist Athos Roussos (whose name and science I also had to look up). The same fog cloaks characters in classics I absorbed growing up: I'm thinking now of the astonishing children in Rebecca West's novel, *The Fountain Overflows.* Yet of all their names I can retain only that of their young cousin, Rosamund, a girl so eerily wise that her name itself has come in my mind to mean preternaturally gifted. I'm not proud of this vagueness of recall, but somehow it doesn't make what those characters gave me less imperishable or dear. While my eyes hold out, I can find them again. James Salter once said something so apt, I've used it for a novel's epigraph: "There comes a time when you realize that everything is a dream, and only those things preserved in writing have any possibility of being real."

A Booth
in the
Marketplace

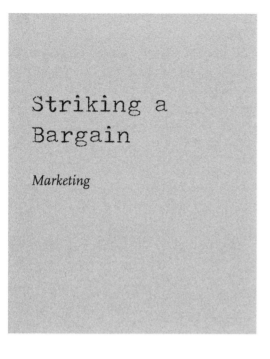

Striking a Bargain

Marketing

Once you've made your work, however long that may take, the moment arrives when you have to offer it up to the world.

It's the completion of the original gesture, the logical parturition. Like any passage, it can prove painful.

What author Thaisa Frank has called "setting up a booth in the marketplace" is difficult to discuss with a level head. Temptation begs me to give in straightaway to yelling—airing private prejudices borne of accrued frustration. Yet I still believe the marketing game can be played with some success by even the least likely among us. Because, in theory, you need not be present to win.

By *win*, I do not mean becoming famous and wealthy (though that is always possible and, rarely, does happen). I mean achieving publication of a worthy work—followed, in best circumstances, by positive critical attention.

Much, so very much, depends on stamina, patience, and drive. A preemptive, good-humored understanding that events tend to devolve to the absurd also helps a great deal. (For example, you travel a far distance, in bad weather, at fair expense, to give a reading where no one shows up.) The rest depends on luck, timing, and cultural climate. The game's been called a lottery for good reason.

■　　■　　■

Marketing one's writing may not be easy for the shy, the solitary, and the sensitive. That's its built-in paradox, of course. Many writers reject the enterprise outright, preferring to live and work quietly, publishing quietly if at all. To most of us, hustling's distasteful at best, at worst on a par with pimping. A personality change seems necessary: many writers find even the concept unsavory. It seems to require acting aggressively, getting "hard," training eyes on the bottom line, the main chance. It means sidelining subtlety in favor of gritty strategizing. It means shutting the door on almost all concerns except those that can help your work.

To bridge the stunning gap between the two phases of making writing, I envision two rooms adjoined by a door. One is the intimate den of Making. This room is private, comforting. It cossets an artist's needs—chaotic or austere, decked with tokens or mattress-lined. The other room, to which the door stays closed until the transitional moment, is the Selling Room.

I think of this room as a Strategic Command Center where big maps cover the table. Target lists and graphs lay about, heavily marked up; several telephones are ringing, coffee's sharp in the air. You change hats here—and personalities. Turning your back upon the tender, private space of making work, you gird in this stripped-down war room for the selling of your writing.

Maybe there's a poster on the wall: a giant photograph of a hand pointing its index finger, Uncle Sam–like, at you, the gazer. Because (oh, how many times must we recall this) you've only yourself to count on in this chaotic business. Unless you've secured an adoring agent or editor, or can afford to hire a year-round, devoted publicist (or several) who will lobby fiendishly for you—and sometimes even *with* all these advantages combined—the final responsibility always falls to you.

Thaisa Frank once told a class that at some point every writer has to decide what bargain he will consent to strike with himself about the marketing of his work. There are levels and trade-offs to consider: what you want, what you're willing to endure. You may choose the athletic exertion of building a "platform" for your books (a publicity-friendly background, website, tie-in events) through agents, publicists, and media flogging: a campaign produced, performed, and promoted by none other than you (with no guarantees of results). Or you may prefer your work be published in modest quantity by a small, independent, or university press. Little money or notoriety attach to these. But small presses often keep their works in print longer, are on occasion reviewed in serious venues, and maintain a sturdy patina of literary respectability.

An article I saw in a writers' magazine called it essential that writers who were determined to help their work's exposure should harness every feasible means, including hiring outside publicists (at something like $5,000 to $15,000 apiece). The piece urged authors to consciously "work" the internet, create a web page, blog their heads off, request that friends review their books online; seek and establish subject and product tie-ins online, attend every gathering (and create some of their own); cultivate editors, publicists, and booksellers; and collect reader contact information for future mass e-mail bulletins. Perhaps worst, the article exhorted writers (in earnestness) *to be thinking and taking notes about subject and product tie-ins while they were in the act of creating their work.*

I felt a terrible sinking dread while reading this, and the cry rose loud in mind and heart:

I didn't become a writer to do these things!

By now you'll know I'm not describing an aversion to work. One works, in my best friend's words, like a Trojan at the writing. But now we are faced with a tandem requirement—a level of promotional zeal that has taken on the gloss of a moral mandate. Writers who object feel cornered by the smug, do-or-die finality: *You want your work to get noticed? Do these things—or watch it go under without a ripple.*

The new reality punches writers between the eyes, and this is when decisions get made about what kind of bargain to strike.

I must believe, in face of all the above, that it is still possible to have a writing life without becoming a brand name or media jockey. That it is possible to carry on writing and get decent critical attention, if not enough lucre to quit the day job. It appears to me that many, many writers—from mid-list to certified obscure—manage to do exactly that.

　　▌　　▌　　▌

Over the years of a writing life, it has also struck me as prudent (if difficult) to distance oneself a bit from particulars of sudden-success stories. You know them. We all hear them: testimonials by people (often distressingly young) who were discovered as undergraduates or waiting tables at Bread Loaf, or by a friend or roommate who knew a highly-placed editor or agent. It's not that these things don't happen; rather that such wunderkind tales can make you feel doomed if you cannot replicate (or have not already replicated) their conditions. This is not to say, don't notice how people got attention. Sometimes you can use such information. But often a success story's gist—*Get lucky like I did*—can further discourage the emerging writer. (Many, including me, will quip they have made a career of *emerging*—been at it too many years to admit.)

My own marketing tactic—for placing stories and books—has been that of the old-fashioned direct-mail campaign. I send work into the world the way children are forced to come of age in a folktale—with a small satchel of food, a few coins, and a tag with their home address sewn under their collars. I wait for the news that they have made good, scanning the blue horizon for a hopeful message floating back. Postal systems and e-mail are my tools. I have relied almost exclusively on the slush pile—that is, offered my work "cold" (uninvited) by surface mail, which is then (as I understand it) piled in huge, wheeled baskets like the ones at the public Laundromat—and there's no doubt that electronic slush amounts to the same thing. This pile is screened and sorted by editorial assistants and interns, underpaid or volunteer young worthies who select promising stuff and send it up the editorial staircase.

In this way, at odd intervals between blizzards of rejection, I have managed to get editors' and agents' attention, and even built relationships with some of them. After years of this, I am, admittedly, tired. My steely can-do armor, which I truly thought indestructible, shows cracks and tarnish. What's most difficult for the unanointed (working writers making careers without benefit of brand-name recognition) is that no sooner is a piece of work taken than the writer starts at the bottom of the hill again, peddling the next. Somehow publication at one level doesn't automatically lead to the next, though you'd imagined it might, and heard stories of how it has. (Likewise, a review in the *New York Times Book Review* does not necessarily provide a golden key.) With rare exception, entrée doesn't seem to accrue, even if you've managed to publish several books.

You need (you are told) to acquire a recognizable Name to gain attention from a major publisher. But how do you get a Name without a major publication?

Once, there probably was a kinder climate toward the up-and-coming writer. There were not so darn many of us then (I am thinking of the mid-century or thereabouts—the Maxwell Perkins to William Shawn zone—when people in positions to extend help, did.) One also imagines the industry was not then quite as hysterically market-driven, or as fragmented by competing modes of media. Katherine Anne Porter could stroll out to her mailbox and drop in a story, and everything would be taken care of for her thereafter; eventually a check would manifest there. Agreed, that's a separate discussion, and it won't fix today's problems. Yet to whatever degree it may have been true, I'm nostalgic for the idea of it.

My attitude toward marketing my work was formed as a child, when I watched my late father going about the business of finding a new teaching job. He acquired telephone books for various cities, I remember, and mowed through them for address information—perhaps he also phoned ahead to gather names and titles. Then he systematically (by mail) queried the colleges he thought first-tier targets for his curriculum vitae. Doubtless he kept checklists and followed up with calls or letters. And by Jove, he found himself a good position fairly quickly. This memory of him—the exhilarating vigor of his attack, the rich fugue of his fingertips flying over the keys at his Royal Portable (my father concertized at the keyboard) with those fat phone books piled around him—pressed itself deeply into my imagination, and as I grew up I copied his method in my searches for schools and jobs. His technique struck me as thoroughly sensible—and a little magical. The gambit seemed to be about *sending a quality of energy out to attract a quality of energy,* and there was always something exciting about going fishing in the serendipity of the Unknown. You folded up your own life with its niggling little sparkles and humbugs, wrapped it snappily, and shot it out into the wide sky as if seeding a cloud with a slingshot—to elicit response from conditions unseen, circumstances you could not actually know much about. There may have been internal shifts in the organizations you'd addressed, just at the time of your query's arrival—say, pregnancies or retirements—that would accidentally open something up in your favor. A department's structure may have changed, responsibilities reconfigured, policies redefined, or moods turned venturesome, keen on bringing in some new blood—or new voices.

That's what you hope for. You can't know what's going on at the other end. It's often best that way. The innocence of your ignorance gives you ballast that is unblemished by political concerns, factionalism, or association with sad events that may have changed internal arrangements. It's good to practice detaching from the results at the time of sending. That way, rejections—even snarky criticisms—won't daunt so badly when they trickle in.

Whereas anything positive—acceptance, praise, encouragement—feels, when it does arrive, like a form of grace or at very least an omen that you're on the right track.

■   ■   ■

A current truth of marketing writing is that it's a fairly ruthless version of musical chairs. Visualize perhaps eight rickety chairs and, say, eight thousand big rear ends skulking around them like the hippopotamus ballerinas in *Fantasia*, hoping to plant themselves in one of those chairs. Publishers are besieged. They are drowning in submissions. If it were possible, they would probably pay you money *not* to submit work to them. Many editors and their aides are young, ambitious, and making their ways toward better situations. Notice how frequently names change on publisher mastheads. Notice how frequently smaller houses dissolve, or are subsumed by larger entities. Yet a few hardy, heroic editors do, somehow, continue to seek and accept and publish new work. So long as that happens, writers continue to scramble to capture their attention.

Like anyone else, I can tell gruesome stories.

I've received declines back from literary journals more than a year later, sometimes as an unsigned form letter, sometimes with a scribbled apology for the delay from a harried editor who explains that things got very crazy. They lost my material. Staff died. Funding stopped. The journal closed. I've sent work to agents and publishers from whom I simply never heard back again.

It used to amaze me that writers received this sort of treatment.

No one speaks of it.

The bigger names keep quietly fulfilling and extending their contracts, and the struggling lesser-known writers keep clawing their way up the castle walls. These latter—by far the majority—are on the begging-bowl end: "the unwashed petitioning the washed," as one blunt literary agent famously phrased it. Another agent admitted to me, sadly: "Nobody wants to talk to writers." One small but admired and well-known publisher sent me a single letter, after many months of holding my (book) manuscript, from someone who signed himself "Bob." It read: "Don't give up. We like your work. Give us a few more weeks." Enthusiastically I wrote Bob at once, telling him I was standing by. Months passed. Neither Bob nor anyone at that publishing house ever wrote again, despite my mailed pleas for any vital sign. Did Bob die?

I believe that writers do not talk about these events because they fear that if they do, they'll be stamped with a scarlet brand— *Whiner*—and carry ever after some plague-like untouchability. They internalize every uncertainty, fearing they have, in some inexplicable way, *caused* their shoddy treatment. It's a ghoulish backstage jungle out there, irrespective of all the gushing magazine articles, seminars, and how-to manuals.

Why should it be like this?

Publishers are in unprecedented crisis: the sextuple-whammy of a devastated economy, flagging revenues, shatter-belt culture, content piracy, shape-shifting formats, and online competition. Most major houses now insist that they will only consider agented work. That puts the burden on the writer to first find a decent agent—someone who believes her work worth the effort of the (nearly insanely upstream) selling process. Agents, for their part, also want to acquire reputations, to impress publishers as heavy-hitters who can recognize (and stand for) bankable work. They want to be taken seriously by reputable houses. And of course they actually hope to make at least a bit of money now and again. It's a free-for-all at every level, with sudden bidding wars flaring up like bushfires between high-end publishers on the slender hunch—a tormenting seed—that a manuscript may "go big."

All of the above should be forgotten as quickly as possible: that is, not allowed to contaminate the autonomous pleasures of the writing life. (This isn't hard. It's so unpleasant that one's delighted to push it away.) The only part a writer need remember is to make good writing, believe in it, and then work one's hind end off. When a book is ready, find a small or university press or get an agent.

I wish I could tell you these processes aren't tough. For a few, they turn out to be a cakewalk. For the rest of us, placing work can prove, again and again, to be the most difficult experience of a writing life.

I keep files of literary agents' rejections. The plan is to be amused by them years from now, perhaps to show friends or classes. All were graceful and shrewd. All asked for my work (in response to my initial query) with near-romantic enthusiasm. Some wanted exclusive consideration, meaning they did not want me to offer a manuscript elsewhere until they'd decided on it. I sent everyone everything. Most kept me waiting for many months and then filled their rejection notes with extravagant regret for taking so much time to deliver a negative verdict—with butter-and-honey praise for my work, which they looked forward to "seeing between hard covers." I knew these people were not required to say nice things about my writing. But it made their rejections more baffling. Why couldn't they take the work, if they admired it so much?

Here is the language, one of a thousand variations: "More and more these days an agent is forced to take on the additional roles of editor and promoter, responsibilities that require vast amounts of time. You deserve an agent who can devote both the passion and the energy that your writing merits. Your manuscript does have a strong and compelling voice—I hope you will persevere until you reach your goal of selling your work and getting it published. As you know, these decisions are largely subjective and another agent will probably be very eager to work with you. I wish you the very best in placing your manuscript."

I've received endless, endless versions of the above statement: my work qualified for the care of a sort of literary Tinkerbell—whom I could only suppose had died long ago from job burnout.

During my first go-round with all this, I was trying to place my first book, a story collection. Quickly, I learned that agents regard story collections as poison. Stories are impossible to sell, agents told me: they (agents, publishers) must first have a novel. I had no novel yet. So I abandoned the search for an agent and began to directly offer my collection to small independents and university presses.

One evening I came home from work to find a fat package waiting on the kitchen table from a small but very reputable press for which I'd held highest hopes. Its editor had loved my story collection, and had sent it to two test readers. This was the last phase of the intake process. After months of chirpy correspondence, the editor had moved past preliminaries and was approaching the final hurdle that was required before recommending the book for publication. If the acquisitions editor loved my manuscript and sent it to readers she picked, what could there now be to fear?

Plenty.

I had waited out those last six weeks of test-reading with confidence. I'd already held a calm dialogue myself about a university press being a perfectly respectable beginning. I'd gone so far as to envision the book's physical appearance and heft; I even had a cover photograph in mind.

Receiving a fat package was not good. Nothing fat should be arriving. Only a slender letter of acceptance.

With unsteady hands I stood at the kitchen table and tore open the thick mailer, the clunky governmental kind that leaks infinitesimal bits of carcinogenic gray stuffing. There was my manuscript and, clipped to its surface, a cover letter typed on the press's official letterhead.

"I am sorry to be the bearer of possible disappointment" were the first words my eyes took in. The words that followed swam in all directions, while my ears roared with *sorry . . . disappointment . . . sorry . . . disappointment*. The rest of the letter was written in the stiff, distanced language of official disengagement, language for the closing of files, with copies to senior staff. It was signed by the acquisitions editor—who, until that moment, had behaved like a fairy godmother.

The two readers she'd selected had found *much to admire* in my book. Dear Lord, how I have come to loathe those words. *Much to admire* always means *I'd rather eat dog food than recommend this material.* The two readers had also, naturally, found much they did *not* admire. The editor included their reports in full, with their names snipped off, of course. One was printed in the typeface of e-mail. (Two full weeks had to pass before I could read through those reports with any clarity, or a regular heartbeat.) Each reader completely contradicted the other, each liking and disliking opposite elements. But the bottom line was that neither could wholly recommend the work for publication. One sounded young and impatient; the other, jokey, familiar, and self-aggrandizing.

Possible disappointment.

(In a later, informal e-mail, the apologetic acquisitions editor admitted that the subjectivity of test readers was the "thorniest aspect" of the intake process—so much so, she said, that she was "amazed any fiction ever got published at all.")

Reader, I had become so convinced publication was going to happen that I can only describe this event as something like getting cracked over the head from behind with a large piece of lumber. I actually found myself running my hand over the back of my head for a day or two, feeling for the lump.

For a few confused days I questioned my ability to make art. Perhaps I truly was not good enough. I had to concentrate to remember a track record: scholarships, awards, grants; colony admissions based on the work. Many fine journals had taken those same stories, individually, that very year. Yet all this evidence felt, at the moment, like it had shrunk to the size of cereal-box trinkets.

My then-fiancé (now husband), to his blessed credit, treated me very gently, insisting we go to dinner and a play that night in a nearby city known for its artistic bravado and bohemianism. All the people I saw that night—boisterous families, earnest singles, distracted waiters in the little Thai restaurant; a studio full of Brazilian Capoeira dancers practicing to the deep thrum of the berimbau; people sipping tea and beer in nearby cafés; the actors onstage, the theater audience, students and workers and elders on the street—seemed so sure of themselves.

I stared at them.

■　■　■

It could end here. But of course it doesn't.

Eventually, another university press took the collection. It was reviewed glowingly in the *New York Times*—Sunday edition, no less.

And then, over the following twenty years, the same Sisyphean ordeal repeated itself with two novels, a second story collection, another novel—and then another.

You're always free to stop. That's the thing.

With the instant wish-fulfillment power of Dorothy's ruby slippers, you can always say you are done, and be done.

Unless you can't.

Unless that's not possible. A strange moment, yes.

Does all this make you stronger? Not really. It makes you bewildered and tired.

But you learn you're unable to quit. At least, so far.

■　■　■

After bouts of serious rejection, it helps to rest and read. Read material that pours warm emollient around your heart. The letters of other artists and writers give comfort. Chekhov's letters. The letters of the late poet Louise Bogan, for the sheer day-to-day clutter and gossip and struggle of that feisty artist's trajectory. Flannery O'Connor's. William Maxwell's to Sylvia Townsend Warner. The letters of Vincent Van Gogh to his brother Theo. How passionately they strived! Vincent wrote his brother this:

> You remember . . . how it happened to Delacroix that 17 pictures of his were refused at the same time. One sees from this . . . that he and others of that period . . . who are rightly called "the valiant," did not call it fighting against hopeless odds, but went on painting. What I [want] to tell you once more, is that if we take that story about Delacroix as a starting-point, we must still paint a lot.

And:

[E]ven in the most refined circles and the best surroundings and circumstances one must keep something of the original character of a Robinson Crusoe or anchorite, for otherwise one has no root in oneself, and one must never let the fire go out in one's soul, but keep it burning.

And especially:

[The word artist] of course include[s] the meaning: always seeking without absolutely finding. . . . As far as I know, that word means, "I am seeking, I am striving, I am in it with all my heart."

Soon after that very first university press rejection, I hobbled back to the desk where my files of target publishers were kept, and resumed the search.

I shut the door to the Making room and quietly sat back down at the Selling table, gazing at maps of the territory.

I scanned a list. Breathing, I began again.

I am seeking. I am striving. I am in it with all my heart.

Reading

Dinosaurs

All I ask of life is the privilege of being able to read.

—William Maxwell

I am seated on the living room carpet with a beer beside my best friend, who is also an author, trading news of writerly struggles. Odds are long; the fiction market, difficult.

Then I tell my friend about another fiction writer, a name much lauded at her debut. Her famous agent, it seems, is not returning her calls.

My friend looks at me pointedly.

"They're scared, you know," she says.

She means agents and editors, gatekeepers of the publishing apparatus.

"Yeah," I say, heart sinking, "I know." I assume she is talking about the stonewalling by publishing circles of literary fiction, also known as the New Hemlock.

But it isn't just fiction sales she is talking about.

"They're scared because we're dinosaurs, you know. Books are dead."

My friend's eyes hold a weird, peevish light, as if to say *dare you to deny it.*

"Not in our lifetimes, of course," she adds, reading the horror in my face.

"But how much have we got left, you and I?" she adds evenly.

My friend's crisp realism would seem misplaced. She's a memoirist, finishing a first novel. Her late father's a beloved, much-championed author and iconoclast. But I know what's firing her conviction. Her twenty-five-year-old daughter, a stunningly gifted young woman who double-majored as an undergraduate in classics and physics, has (at this writing) recently completed a special graduate studies program in computer game design. My stepson, twenty-four, is one of the girl's lifelong pals. He's finished college, is serenely fluent in Spanish, and seeks work with public policy and developing countries. Both young adults are kind, just, superbly educated, and (all biases aside) tremendously, deeply smart. Neither reads many books these days—or rather, fewer and fewer, as they distance themselves from conventional schools. They get most of their information online. In point of fact, most of their young lives have been spent online. It's simply a way of life for them, as it is for their peers, and for the generations to follow. They've played every game, and my friend's daughter is now inventing and designing new ones. They believe that computer games can be educative and moral. My friend is thrilled for her daughter's prospects. I'm thrilled that my friend is thrilled, and thrilled her daughter is happy and fruitful and able to plan for a bountiful future. But (may lightning not strike me now, please) I can't, in my inmost heart, care much about computer games— neither in reality nor for their potential, however meaningfully intended. All they seem to involve is a protagonist hopping (or trudging) through difficulty; only the settings change. (Granted, that description may offer a greater parallel with literary novels than I'm happy to admit.) My friend's daughter will probably one day start a games-design company and make terrific money. I'm truly glad for this young woman, as I say, and for my friend. We want our kids to thrive and prosper and contribute.

But for the love of heaven, I want to plead, *don't take books away.* Except with what, or whom, do I plead?

My friend's face, watching the blood leave mine, holds firm. Her expression says *I know you hate this. I don't love it either. But we both know it's true, and beyond our control.* She's begun to witness it firsthand. She teaches at our city's community college. Her classes don't, or won't, read books, or much else. My own husband, a veteran teacher at the same college, has long-ago grasped that his classes don't read. None of his students knew who Ernest Hemingway was, when he asked. They don't know who Martin Luther King was, or where anyplace is on a map. They are eighteen, nineteen, twenty years old. My husband had supposed that in high school, someone might have placed some of the above information before their eyes. Or that they might have seen a headline or wondered who the holiday was named for.

Alas.

My friend tries to jolly me, the way you shake a toy in front of a baby. Soon, she explains, a futuristic device will not only contain bunches of downloaded books—it will project text onto ceilings or walls so a reader won't even have to sit up or turn a page. I'm sickened by the idea. I don't want to read from walls or a screen, or the backs of my own eyeballs. I want to read from the bound paper pages held in my hands.

But once, it is also true, I dreaded the internet. Now I'm uneasy without access to it every day of my life.

Dizziness begins snaking through me, as I envision time dissolving the cultural structures we've always banked our assumptions against. Down they go like cliffs of sugar, fast and loose, no matter what anyone says or does. In my own life, computers evolved from mainframes the size of rooms to small shiny cases thinner than a dinner mint, cell phone technology refined the same way, cathode ray to digital, films to DVD, reel-to-reel audiotape to cassette to CD. But books would never leave. I was certain of that. A hardy, rebel underground (what Paul Auster has called "a secret club") would always tunnel along beneath whatever else went on, exchanging books and dialogue.

But if the young have no interest—that is, if their interest goes elsewhere—that underground will die. Then "books" will become another entry in the online glossary of archaic terms, like "harpsichord." And everyone will walk around toting their text-projection devices. Or perhaps those will be replaced by implanted chips: scan a wrist or an eye past an electronic sensor and written work will be projected inside the mind or spoken into what was once known as the reading ear.

We can urge the young to read, and untold thousands of adults still work passionately to instill love of books in their curious, lively kids. But I can't help sense an awful futility seeping through. It's a peculiar experience to feel checkmated by time, and by the evidence of trends you've witnessed with your own eyes.

Robert Gottlieb, venerated editor of *The New Yorker* and Alfred A. Knopf (and first-rate writer and biographer), said this to Laura Miller, of the online site Salon:

> I can't tell you how many times we've buried the book in my lifetime. The fact is that we haven't buried the book, and however all this works out, we're still not going to be burying the book. People are still going to be reading books, and whether they're going to be reading them on a Kindle or as a regular physical hardcover book or a paperback or on their phones or listening to audiobooks, what's the difference? A writer is still sending his or her work to you, and you're absorbing it, and that's reading.

I'm trying to remember his words. Of course there's no other available answer, except to keep reading and writing. To hungrily track reviews and conversations. To hold the books—all those real, physical, bound and glued paper pages I've ever read or hope to read—hold them close and high, with an eye toward the incoming tide.

Underwhelmed
and Eccentric

Though the love of earnest literature and all it stands for appears to shrink daily, giving way instead to a kind of homogenized sludge of recipes, travelogues, horror serialists and the like, all meted out with equal chirpiness at the same shrink-wrapped sale—I suppose we are lucky to live in a place where it is still possible to keep eccentric tastes and habits and remain legal.

In short, we can still be cranks about what we read, and why.

And as years and contexts pass, it appears to me that some writers may have but a few numinous books or stories in them; that these works may bubble up (or be mined, painfully) during a particularly fertile slice of writing life—and that the writers may find themselves thereafter faced with the odd problem of following their own magical act.

It is those early, lesser-sung books that speak to me, that belong to a special category—and with them, long-standing old classics which by now may be taken for granted. To me this soft substratum exists as a kind of secret ore for a secret club: readers who deliberately wander the thrilling, illogical, underground world of slightly-obscure discoveries.

I've kept this queer superstition since childhood, when I rifled the dusty shelves of the tiny local library (someone's old splintery house) every week in Sunnyslope, Arizona. Somehow I knew even then that *the sleeper was the thing.* The unobtrusive, quiet *Nobody's Boy* and *Nobody's Girl* (popular in France but little-known here), by Hector Malot, were likelier in my ratings system than, say, *Black Beauty* to strike me as strange and unique, to enchant and disturb, suggesting half-glimpsed worlds that would take me far away. I found a rhythm for ferreting them out—rapid scanning, like leafing through clothing in bargain outlets—then carried my treasure home as furtive and roused as any shoplifter. Assured of entering a series of agreeable spells, I could anticipate floating outside earth-time for a while, unable to pull my head from each book until it was finished. And even if I "forgot" the book on the surface of consciousness, I knew it would somehow continue to live in me.

As a young adult I came to practice similar voodoo, scanning shelves with the same weird radar. I tended to look for trade paperbacks in musty little bookstores, titles often first published by small, iconoclastic concerns like City Lights, Black Sparrow, Calyx, and Sun & Moon, or old imprints like Touchstone and Poseidon, and braver, once-established houses like Mercury House and North Point. So many of these are gone now. Many valiantly delivered the book-child before themselves perishing in the birth process. Their very names only added to the sense that the book was a partially-obscured jewel.

In this way I met and fell secretly in love with (to toss a random handful of glitter) Gina Berriault, Laurie Colwin, Lorrie Moore, Paul Auster, James Agee, Christopher Tilghman, Ursula Hegi, Marilynne Robinson, Richard Rhodes, Rachel Ingalls, Thaisa Frank, Lucia Berlin, and John Williams (for his astonishing, unforgettable *Stoner*). Among the late elders, I recall seeking out Edmund Gosse, Edith Wharton, Ivan Turgenev, Jane Austen,

Henry James, and Gustave Flaubert (*Sentimental Education* before *Madame Bovary*). Among international moderns, names like J. L. Carr, Annie Ernaux, Edna O'Brien, Natalia Ginzburg, Mavis Gallant, Virginia Woolf, Cesare Pavese, Primo Levi, Marguerite Yourcenar, Jean Rhys, Isak Dinesen, Penelope Fitzgerald, and Anne Michaels still quicken my pulse a few beats.

Now I am older, and have watched subsequent writings from many of these marvelous authors, living or dead, gain popular attention. The living writers may go on to produce loads of work. All of it may be gobbled, respectfully reviewed, and made into movies, the writer's name may be pressed into the pantheon, and the writer may grow revered and *au courant*—on rare occasion at a level with rock stars and filmmakers. Glossy magazines smelling of high-end cologne may vie with privately-funded literary quarterlies for that writer's next pages, if only a bit of commentary or elliptical sketch.

In short, the writer becomes commodified.

And at this point, perhaps unfairly, I lose interest. It may have to do with knowing too much: the maker has taken the spotlight; the cheese stands alone. She may still be questing the good quest, doing worthy work—but for me, what matters is done. The special, juicy, miraculous thing was made, and stands. The work, which tapped into a somehow familiar mystery and raised the fine hairs along arms and backs of necks, has happened—and won't repeat.

I have puzzled about this for years because, as a writer and reviewer, I witness intelligent people trying to define and defend a coherent valuation of writing. I follow reviews (and write some of them), watching the titans battle it out to decide the ultimate merits of contemporary giants in venues like the *New York Review of Books* or the *Times Literary Supplement*. Yet among these best minds, little emerges that's conclusive. They may influence what is published, what is rewarded with grants and prizes, and they may vitalize the literary roundtable. But the basic chemistry of reading remains obstinately, perennially, eccentrically one-on-one: that of writing to reader.

In part to escape my small town's suburban dailiness, I used to commute once a month to a nearby city to attend a reading group, the rules of which were chaotically loose. Range in taste was wide. But I noticed that when a book's author was no longer living (say, Colette) or was otherwise remote to the group's fairly mainstream readers (say, William Kotzwinkle), if members disliked the writing, they didn't hesitate to declare it. If, however, the book was a follow-up to a big splash made by a contemporary writer they knew, or knew of (say, Ethan Canin), or whose integrity they admired (say, Dorothy Allison), I saw real unwillingness in my friends' eyes to say *this held no magic for me.* I saw them underwhelmed and casting around for ways not to say so.

In those instances I sensed we were not squaring off with the purpose of reading, which is never anything less than the present-tense miracle of persuasion. The book we'll forever remember is the dream that lands in the middle of our harried, exhausted lives like a *Close Encounters* spaceship. Unfurling its little beam-of-light staircase, it bids us enter, seals itself up with us in it, and soars away.

I think readers have a right to say a work misses that. Not in order to be churlish, but to keep critical equilibrium by stating the case—that for whatever reason the writing does not enfold us into its dream. I listened to that book group fuss over the likelihood of various details of plot or character as if the plausibility of the whole project turned on whether Auntie Mollie *really would have* driven down to Texas and taken up with Enrique. It felt as if, once certain tiny engineering errors were fixed, even theoretically, the whole contraption would achieve liftoff—and ease my friends' consciences.

As a writer, I am humbled by the mystery of craft, the mechanics of persuasion; I am never entirely sure these can be taught and systematically applied—though I've been lucky to work with gifted teachers, and though it seems possible to learn to avoid common errors and gain insight that way. Still, it is comforting to me that we can never make a provable, hard pronouncement about where good writing comes from, or what ultimately makes it charged and memorable.

We can, however, always feel entitled to a *sanctity of private response* to writing. After all, that's the igniting spark that brings us to this under-loved avocation in the first place. And so it falls to us, in the course of responding to work, to protect that right: to resist the bullying of market hype, of zeitgeist favor or disfavor, and (perhaps most trickily, most insidiously) of obligation to writing peers.

■   ■   ■

Tastes rage and change. Culture approves or rejects. An author may not like or understand her own work's impact. Or she may try hard to make a thunderous impact and succeed, or not. Every variable is feasible—some simultaneously. So when another well-educated friend complained that a famous writer underwhelmed him, despite avalanches of cultural praise, I could only shrug. The fact of misplaced or disproportionate cultural adoration (and the social forces that urge it) is a permanent one. It is something every writer has to come to terms with, something unlikely to alter even if some well-meaning zealot takes it on himself to broadcast passionate, brilliant rebuttals around the clock in a blitz of truth-in-advertising—or insists that all publishers attach disclaimer labels: "Caution: the following pages may not embody the degree of quality suggested by reviews, blurbs, and hearsay."

The late critic Julien Gracq calmly declared that we tend to judge writers according to "extra-literary factors: physical or moral prestige, membership in a group, friends, lovers, a sparkling biography, a historical or political role"—in effect, "through the eyes of their time." It seems we've no choice.

And yet we've all experienced the distress that friends and media can wreak when they've primed us to experience a work as better than it is: "What, am I crazy?" (Though tastes can coincide, thank heaven. I remember a writing teacher saying of an Alice Munro story I was about to study, "If you don't wind up liking this story *I'll buy you a car.*" He was right. "Carried Away" has electrified and haunted me ever since. Alas!) Nonetheless, it consoles me that finally, whatever the outside influence, the chemistry of books remains stubbornly intimate. As with a love affair, politics and family can exert some sway. But if the charge is missing (and you aren't living in an old-world dynasty of arranged marriages), you move on.

(Timing, however, still counts. There were periods when I simply could not enter *To the Lighthouse* or *War and Peace*. Years later I slipped into them, rapturous, without a ripple.)

So I defend the idiosyncratic rhythm of discovery. The list of books and writers that have consumed me, and that I've in turn assimilated, is ragged and chaotic. (For a wonderful series of titles in this vein, see Lynne Sharon Schwartz's *Ruined by Reading* or Francine Prose's glossary of titles in *Reading Like a Writer*.) My list would doubtless make some readers sniff, "Huh! Old hat. Pedestrian." Others might wonder what fussy arcana I am talking about. Still others would declare I've missed the truly important works entirely. Authors who pierce us for the first-and-for-all time may be long gone (Homer) or lately arrived (C. E. Morgan, Simon Van Booy, Justin Torres); timeless icons (Tolstoy) or one-time brilliant flashes (Harper Lee). Significance is shaped by timing and context.

Part of the joy of the hunt—which you effect, ironically, by trying not to try too hard—is in finding the next one. Because I'm no longer young, I must now conduct that process with an attitude of mystical determinism, trusting that during my lifetime I will meet up with the books that will be important, even as I must gracefully allow that I will never know the wealth of the best-read—those who've had the luxury or drive to absorb the cream of literature over a lifetime.

⁑ ⁑ ⁑

Nothing can really follow—in the sense of equally match—the impact of the dream that comes to stay. And nothing *should* follow it. Instead, each dream should take root for itself, a secret germination over the rest of our days, seeping into identity. Whenever possible, it is good to read writers before they become vaunted—or a long while after. Good to seek out work that proves at once to be its own best thing, for no other reason than how the first page whispers to you, or because someone pulls at your sleeve with *that look* in their eyes and declares *you must read this*, or because you saw an old essay somewhere praising the writer. With little fanfare its impact is truly private, as if inside a velvet-curtained voting booth, tumbling directly into the whirling gears of the attentive reader's mind and heart.

Artists do what they can, as they can. Some blessed few cannot help continually spilling gold. Some know the right people. The rest of us will produce more unevenly, thankful for a turn at the booth in the marketplace. The pace of a writer's progress must proceed in deliberate exile from a society's relentless measuring and grading, filtering and retrenching. And as a sort of logical parallel, the passionate (eccentric) reader really has no choice but to seek that elusive mutual osmosis with each work, believing—each time—in a certain mystery necessary to the seeking process. Holding reviews at bay, holding gossip at bay, we hold out for the random, tender, slightly obscure collision with the one-time miracle of a beautiful book.

A Hand in
the Game

Reviewing

Plenty of writers make a point of exempting themselves (perhaps *recusing* is the better word) from reviewing other writers' work.

I understand this.

They (the self-recused) can't expunge the painful awareness of how long it takes to make a book; how much of their own blood and bits of chopped-up internal organs were invested in their books (along with all the glass shards); how hopelessly personal, and therefore vulnerable to outsider assessment, the project will always be. To deliver a public judgment on someone else's work strikes them as resembling a choice to stroll into oncoming traffic—asking for bad juju regarding the critical reception of their own work.

Most authors have lived through at least a couple of bad reviews. Helplessness figures as a key component in one's first response to these. The reviewer's word, in most cases, is final.

One can't strike back. Of course one could if one chose, with an outraged letter (or a punch in the nose at the next possible chance), but nearly everyone understands that it's terrible form to do so. Even if such a letter is matchlessly wise and the writer a star, a strange air of non-consequence hangs in the ozone after the letter's appearance, along with the faintly comic tang kicked up by the spectacle of clashing egos in any field (no matter how famous or furious), partly because the fuss is delimited by that field. The non-relevance to the average outsider makes the fracas seem like infighting; we lift an amused brow at the tiffs between geneticists or astrophysicists, and so on. In any case, the Unspoken Writers' Integrity Code (my label) stipulates that after receiving a bad review a writer had best vanish noiselessly back down her prairie dog hole—presumably to try again.

Novelist Richard Russo noted to the *New York Times Book Review*, alongside his first book review for them in eighteen years:

> I don't review books very often . . . which is odd because I love to talk about them. The problem is that I don't have much interest in discussing books I don't like. It takes me four or five years to write a novel, and no matter how much I may hate a book, I can't get out of my head the fact that some poor schlemiel worked lovingly on it for a very long time. A movie producer friend of mine once remarked that most people have no idea how hard it is to make even a bad movie, and I feel the same way about novels. I don't dispute that it's somebody's job to blow the whistle on bad books, bad movies, bad art. It's just not mine if I can help it.

Richard Ford seconded that vote: "Giving a colleague a bad review is like driving down the road, seeing a hitchhiker and rather than picking the hitchhiker up, you run over him." Nonetheless, peruse the pages of the *Times Book Review* or any other major reviewing venue, and you'll note that most reviewers are themselves authors of serious reputation. Most of them make calm, sane work of it. A few happen to be terrific writers. One pays close attention to them. (Being an excellent writer does not guarantee reviewing acumen, but it enhances the odds.) I have never asked writing friends why they review; the reasons probably seem too obvious to them to elucidate. But if energy and conviction are any indication, their decision to review seems an untroubled one. I would bet a great deal that if writers *did* name their reasons—payment's too modest to count—those reasons would resemble my own. Here are some of them:

A hand in the game, a voice in the conversation. To think and talk about reading and writing is delicious luxury. When I shape a review, I feel that I am shaping an intimate message (as if over a café table) about something whose survival matters desperately to both the listener and me—not just the book at hand, but the cause of literary art. It's exhilarating, too, to be trusted by editors with a valuable patch of public space (online or on paper) in which to make my case. Part of that trust is their assumption of some authority on my part. It compels me to rise to their expectations. I give the effort swaths of time and ferocious attention.

Visibility. There are but a few ways to help one's name recur in places perused by literature-friendly eyes. Many writers prefer to blog, as a method of connecting to a reading public. But because there's such an avalanche of them now, it strikes me that much individual blogging, however gifted, wafts unread into the ether. Nonetheless, as more and more journalism migrates to online status, book reviewing venues may soon be exclusively accessed that way, and continue to draw the faithful.

Reviewing forces a writer to read against type. A reviewer must read what she is assigned. Often these will be titles she'd not likely choose for herself. *Tant mieux.* Opening wide the reading-intake gates allows a reviewer to learn more about the industry during any given period: what's being offered, what it's made of, and whether that offering is sufficiently honored or appreciated (or over-honored). Even if the going proves difficult and she finds she doesn't care for the assignment, she will gain useful perspective, as well as a crash course in deploying diplomatic language.

Reviewing forces a writer to clarify and re-clarify values. The late, esteemed John Updike created a list of (blessedly sane) suggestions for reviewers, opening with what may be the single most important: "Try to understand what the author wished to do, and do not blame him for not achieving what he did not attempt." Further: "Do not imagine yourself a caretaker of any tradition, an enforcer of any party standards, a warrior in an ideological battle, a corrections officer of any kind." That does not mean, however, that a reviewer should not apply all her heart and mind to the job.

Reviewing offers the chance to communicate a passion for reading. The possibility of igniting that passion in others drives one's efforts. Updike notes, mildly enough: "Submit to whatever spell, weak or strong, is being cast. . . . The communion between reviewer and his public is based upon the presumption of certain possible joys in reading, and all our discriminations should curve toward that end." It will surprise no one that those joys occur in the process of discovery—as they will for any alert reader. These happen, thank heaven, with heartening regularity. The difficulties, of course, arrive when a reviewer is disappointed or dismayed by what she finds. She must discuss her reservations in print without trashing the work outright. Trashing it will serve no one and take the cause of literature down a peg. One owes readers honesty. If a work is so unpalatable that a reviewer feels she'll have to lie to say anything nice about it, she should return the book to her editor with that declaration.

Have I made mistakes? Lord, yes. I've overpraised work out of caution. Joe Queenan brilliantly mocked this phenomenon, shaming nearly every reviewer down to her shoe soles, in an essay for the *Times Book Review*. Blunt as a hammer, Queenan noted that "the vast majority of book reviews are favorable, even though the vast majority of books deserve little praise," and that "even if one reviewer hates a book, the next 10 will roll over like pooches and insist it's not only incandescent but luminous, too." He suggested that reviewers err in this direction because they fear "reprisals down the road." Exactly what form might those reprisals take? Making a lot of enemies may be the most delicate description.

Of course I remember—flinching—the pronouncements of reviewers who assessed my own work uncharitably. But a friend wisely reminded me that I can now claim membership in a big club: like bearing that oddly-shaped vaccine stamp on the upper arm.

Do I scramble to read reviews, consulting them first thing each day like racing forms, sifting, mulling, grim and intense as any junkie? I do. Does one learn to read between lines, to ascertain by the deft diction of courteous professionals whether a work is worth one's time? Absolutely. Does one learn by default, and by a kind of literary chivalry, to produce that code oneself? Alas, yes. Is that practice good for literary culture? Probably not. Is the reviewing industry often arbitrary, uneven, unrigorous, over-craven toward names and publishers, stuffed with cronyism, feuds, favor culling, and back-scratching? Of course it is. Is it better than nothing? It has to be. Literary venues are fighting for their lives.

An entire book devoted to the problematic state of contemporary reviewing, called *Faint Praise,* by reviewer and editor Gail Pool, provides as thoroughgoing and crisp an analysis as one may desire.

Has anyone admired its ideas enough to implement them?

Well—*Kirkus* and *Publishers' Weekly* liked it just fine.

Enough with
the Change
and Growth

*[I]n contrast to [X], . . . who genuinely
evolves in the course of [another] novel
and achieves a kind of self-knowledge,
[Y] never emerges as . . . someone who
learns or changes or grows.*

So pronounced a famous reviewer, in a famous American newspaper's book review section a few years ago, assessing a new novel
by a respected author.

And I stared at her words, which sounded, in my reading ear,
petulant and scornful. And I continue to wonder: *Why must a
character change and grow?*

In what code of literary laws was it written? Does human life
reflect interior transformation often enough to warrant this
event's predictable popping up, like timed toast, in modern literature? Surely not. How many inner transformations do you notice
in friends and family as a general rule? So what is it with this
compulsion of ours?

Why does modern literary fiction (and, frequently, nonfiction)
seem bound by cultural contract to depict at least one character
undergoing a soulful sea change?

Maybe our stories would otherwise be too boring. Maybe it's a fantasy held dear. Or a carryover from the mores of a fable-oriented history, where some facsimile of happy ending, lesson learned, or message or moral, is so longed for that if readers must forgo it, we demand the door-prize consolation of (at least) a few choice realizations. Or maybe the change and growth mandate provides a brand of entertainment—since learning and growing tend, realistically, to be erratic, quiet, and rarely guaranteed to last.

Maybe it's just plain wishful thinking. Charles Baxter, in a brilliant essay against literary epiphanies, suggests an economic interpretation: "For the middle class . . . insights can lead to a sense of how things work and how they may be controlled." Drily, he notes: "The epiphany was never meant to be used for merchandising and therapy." Nonetheless, "[t]he job has been done. . . . Just because there is no religion around doesn't mean that the rest of us aren't under intense pressure to be saved these days, not when there is so much money to be made in the saving of us."

Whatever its reason, I'd like to argue for a moratorium among reviewers and (otherwise) bright readers on their dogged insistence that contemporary writing be measured against this tired notion. There seems a stubborn need, among reviewers anyway, to locate that turn in a given work—almost to race for it, as if diving for the wrapped trinket in a box of Crackerjacks. One begins to suspect literature won't be considered literature in present terms unless it leads the pronouncers to a recognizable, epiphanic payoff. Now, payoff, which is a fairly vulgar term for reader satisfaction or nourishment—reminding us of a gumball or slot machine—is a familiar concept in the study of craft. Payoff may be delivered, technically, by any number of elements—place, theme, style, tone, and so forth. But lately this foot-tapping, watch-consulting expectation of a character's *aha* moment, demanded so often and so indignantly by reviewers who (one imagines) should know better, knocks on its ear the original idea of the *venture* of writing, the investigation that drives it, the idea that a writer often embarks on a novel or story hardly knowing where she's going, hoping to find out mainly by getting there—that sturdily mysterious process of one image or word leading to the next and the next. And considered in that light, the sensibility requiring reliable character change and growth feels, to me, like insistence on a recipe, to those students who stop their creative writing teacher—in this case, a friend of mine—to ask: "But when do we put in the symbolism, Mrs. Gardiner?"

Of course it's not wrong or uncommon for a character to come to self-knowledge, or to a newer or larger comprehension. Works across centuries are consummated by these instances, and it's certainly one of the reasons we read. Nor can we deny that art makes a shape and a substance from the chaos of life that must, by the very nature of taking form, elide and organize and distill material in ways that life can't. And of course, modes of storytelling evolve and shift over time. But as any grown-up (and many pre-grown-ups) may observe, things work complicatedly among and within the humans of our world. And if in literature we aim to frame off and consider some of those workings, then surely they deserve to be depicted, within the given form, as faithfully as possible.

Sometimes a reader's payoff consists of realizing that nothing much will happen—that characters won't (or can't) change or learn or grow, that certain characters will never come to terms, that various elements, internal and external, won't allow it. But that understanding itself proves enlarging. And that's what is undervalued, or missed outright, too often, by many reviewers.

I can't claim expertise. But I'm conversant with a long, fond tradition in literature (especially American) of characters' arriving to greater knowledge or awareness—from the most exquisitely subtle versions to the neon-lit billboard variety. The range of those *aperçus* is too vast to address here—from "when I became a man, I put away childish things," to "Reader, I married him," to "Aunt Sally she's going to adopt me and sivilize me, and I can't stand it. I been there before," to myriad modern examples. We're deeply affected by what befalls those characters with whom we've traveled. We've taken in their news. What becomes apparent in time is that news tends to show its face in the course of contained movement, like that of a wristwatch. Such movement may be so subtle as to seem nearly imperceptible. But a good work allows us to detect it, absorb it, come to understand it and be affected by it ever after.

Sometimes that movement is a matter of a lovely relationship's deepening. (Yoko Ogawa's *The Housekeeper and the Professor*.) Sometimes it monitors the trajectory of a ruinous relationship worsening. (Raymond Carver.) Sometimes it's a meditation on a framed segment of fictive time. (Peter Handke's *The Afternoon of a Writer*.) Sometimes it's pure remembrance—when things aren't learned so much as noted: the strangeness of individuals arbitrarily given to us as family; the implacable dramas of our pasts. I'm oversimplifying, but the idea should be apparent: characters do what they must according to who they are, what or who acts upon them, the confines and currencies of the worlds they inhabit, and so on. I wouldn't dream of wondering when, like symbolism or toast, change and growth were going to appear. I only ask to be held by the story's voice and taken where it has to go.

"Literature," Baxter reminds us, "is not an instruction manual."

So why does a smart reviewer demand that a character demonstrate change and growth as though she (the reviewer) were checking off items on a list of matriculation criteria? Her irritation suggests that if no change and growth have shown up, the story has been pointless—that nothing else about the writing swooped in and gave the story its right to exist. That may have been the case with the novel she spoke of, which I've not read. But I sense that many readers have been conditioned to seek some sort of moral milestone in a character's journey (to the exclusion of much else) as a way of confirming they "got good weight" for their investment—that they'll have learned something along with the character without having had to endure the character's pain and risk—a kind of vitamin, or catharsis by proxy. In that view, the whole act of reading does triple-duty, offering distraction and entertainment while slipping the medicine down.

Oh, we do love to multitask. And we love those self-help models.

"Heedlessness in a character is not interesting," comments my husband when I describe my frustration with the snippy book reviewer. He is a playwright, and has his own criteria-demons to wrestle. Granted, a heedless character—in my husband's meaning, one who's stone-oblivious to whatever's acting upon him—may not compel. But a character's heedlessness only forms one strand of the tapestry. Who is it, say, in *Long Day's Journey into Night*—or in a Chekhov story—that arrives with sorrow and compassion to the knowledge, in the course of the story's movement, that the ensemble before us will only speed up its swan dive into the abyss? We viewers. We readers.

Playwright Sarah Ruhl has remarked: "The Aristotelian model—a person wants something, comes close to getting it but is smashed down, then finally gets it or not, then learns something from the experience—I don't find helpful. It's a strange way to look at experience." And Flannery O'Connor said: "A story always involves, in a dramatic way, the mystery of personality."

My gut sense, from listening to contemporaries and reading reviews, is that readers, especially Americans, don't do well with that mystery, with open-endedness—however powerful a quality of *inevitability* may also be driving things. It leaves many with what they might call "a bad feeling." They'd prefer their stories, if you please, in a clean, tight container, with no surprise ingredients or weird aftertastes. Redemption, like a bright cherry plunked on top, would be dandy. Are these preferences a crime? If readers agree to dwell awhile with dissonance, darkness and complexity, might it be their reasonable right to demand a few comforting amenities in return?

I'd offer: *Look closer. They may already be there.*

It's always dangerous to talk about serious literary endeavor by the lights of popular taste. There's tension between the passion of the maker, who's had to follow her mystery, and the earnest efforts of the reader, who wishes to make sense of what she's grasping. Thank heaven, now and again a collaboration across this tension succeeds, and succeeds joyfully. Pulitzer Prize winner Elizabeth Strout's terrific story cycle *Olive Kitteridge* features an eponymous character who's as obstreperous and truculent and change-resistant as they come. Does Olive really alter in the course of bashing herself (in anger, anguish, and sorrow) against people and events? My sense of it was that by its closing, certain odd adjustments did indeed begin to occur inside that embattled, spiky woman. And the act of witnessing this *works* something in a reader, an acute awareness it would almost violate to attempt to name. Perhaps the last word—effectively silencing even a critic of the critics, conferring a shrewd challenge and a blessing too—should be Strout's, who reminded a roomful of readers not long ago: "Olive belongs to *you* now."

Imposed Yet Familiar

Defending the Memoir

$\mathcal{S}$yndicated columnist Ellen Goodman bemoaned, years ago, what was then seen as a sort of national literary rash: the Invasion of the Memoirs.

"Today, the memoir's the thing," she wrote. "In this country . . . the first person trumps the third person in publishing. . . . [T]he hottest writing workshops are now called 'Memoirs.' Many of our most accomplished novelists . . . are finding wider audiences for the stories of their real lives. . . . Memoirists have taken over the cultural role of storyteller, secret sharer. . . . It's easier," she sighed, "to put an author on tour than a main character."

Goodman's distress signal was not the first. A number of high-profile journalists took up arms—or eyebrows—over a surge of literary works in memoir form, citing *Angela's Ashes, The Kiss, The Liar's Club,* and myriad other titles. Protesters argued that fiction, which presumably required more imaginative work to penetrate, assimilate, and value, was being bypassed for the shallower, gaudier bimbo called the memoir. They fretted that the memoir could not *mean* as deeply or as well as fiction; that it constituted junk food, spoiling reader appetites for the true, long-term nourishment to be gained—or was it earned?—through the novel.

The argument struck me, then and now, as specious. At its best, autobiographical literature can embody an art to reckon with. It can console, help form and inform us all our days. Who'd disallow that?

Goodman's complaint was triggered when an Australian author revealed that a popular, prizewinning memoir of an Aboriginal girl had in fact been his work of fiction. Unable to sell it as fiction (allegedly because he was a white male), he had peddled it instead as memoir, with instant success. While the hoax is interesting and perhaps lamentable (and has been repeated several times since then with other notorious titles), the reality it apparently underscores is the memoir genre's cachet. The author "hit the literary jackpot because he switched genres, not genders," quipped Goodman. And that is what her article went on to deplore.

Vilifiers of the memoir's ballooning popularity may fear there is not enough money or recognition to go around. Even if that's true, it's hard to imagine high culture's frown rerouting market trends. Money for writing is always a lottery. Bidding wars among publishers, which feed advances to writers as if placing bets on racehorses, have long been notorious for their frantic obsessions. Are we witnessing, as Goodman supposed, a sudden "failure of the culture's imagination"? Surely there's been nothing sudden about it. Television, with its heartless laugh tracks and complexity-free plotlines, has been nursing the imagination-deprived for over sixty years.

Goodman wrote: "At the logical end of this [pro-memoir] reasoning lies the terrible idea that we cannot trust anyone to understand or speak for anyone else." I take her point, but gently note we Americans are too numerous, and too crude, to provide an accurate measure. We're too scattershot to manage that much coherence. If we have rushed out and proved our preference by spending tons of money on *Angela's Ashes,* we have also rushed out and spent a ton more on *The Bridges of Madison County* and *The Da Vinci Code* and the *Twilight* series. Sales, from which Goodman and colleagues reckon, reflect popular taste, not creeds. People don't entertain creeds anymore (if they ever did), exempting maybe the stubborn "I know what I like." People waiting in superstore checkout lines are not harboring a burning philosophical conviction about the innate superiority of one or another literary form. John Grisham won't lure them away from Tolstoy.

Anyway, fiction's alive. Best-seller lists still bubble with it. Classics, against nearly insane odds, still sell, Austen to Zola. Waves of MFAs in fiction flood the nation's English and creative writing departments—in my region, hundreds of hyperqualified individuals apply for a single available teaching position. Meanwhile, the slush piles and in-boxes of every vehicle for fiction grow slushier. Form rejection notices from these overwrought journals pour back to the writerly wannabes like a reverse tide, their messages pleading: "We filled our fiction quota months ago. Try next year!"

One teacher I know worries about the threat of the memoir coming to be "mistaken" for "real" literature, arguing that great fiction offers a quality of context, pith, and meaning that memoirs do not. Again, it seems wrongheaded to force a contest. The best memoirs, to me, provide a kind of literary sibling to fiction, blood kin but separate in features and characteristics. And it makes no more sense to demand that one form best itself against the other than to square the sun off against the moon. We can fight all day about what is and is not the "purest" literature (and we haven't yet considered the blatantly autobiographical novel or the intensely novelistic memoir). But what or whom would anyone's bloody victory serve?

I suspect that the real impetus of resentment stems in part from a universal impulse which both admires and begrudges quick success. The circuit of academics and writers known better to each other than to the reading populace at large both covets and distrusts what prospers commercially, as public acclaim is still (somewhere in our hearts) suspected to contaminate the sacred literary, over which we have long slung the ascetic's sackcloth. Thus, if your memoir appears on the best-seller list, it may be a cheesier product and you a crafty manipulator of profit-making hype—or not. But if that hype apparatus is in place anyway—and of course it is—why not let it occasionally welcome (as it will) the remarkable to its ranks and bump off some of the genuine louts on board? This event needn't tarnish fiction's high standing; in fact, it might bring that standing closer to public scrutiny by default. Former Poet Laureate Robert Hass commented to me in an interview (italics mine):

> I think any art that doesn't have popular roots is in trouble. So the fact that there's a whole range of kinds of writing doesn't seem like a problem. . . . What could be wrong with it? A lot of bad poetry? There's always been a lot of bad poetry. *But it seems like during periods when people take an interest in art, [art] thrives.* In the Tong Dynasty, when everybody had to write poems in order to get a job in the civil service bureaucracy, it produced eight of the great lyric poets of the world. Big boom in the novel as a popular art form, you get Tolstoy and Dostoevsky. Big boom in theatre in the new emergent cities, you get Shakespeare. Film, Chaplin. And so on.

I want here to vouch for the importance of the memoir form, for its durable art and mystery, and for the fact that in the mind and heart of the literary omnivore, it simply compounds (rather than compromises) the sum of wonderful literature, squiring fiction like a nutritional coeval.

▪   ▪   ▪

Taste and judgment evolve, as does quality of character (or so we hope), over time, with experience. There were periods while I was growing up when I badly needed to see how various others had met or failed to meet the shocks and bafflements of life, how they'd dug for the bone of meaning, and how they'd made or lost their ways. Nothing could quite speak to me then like first-hand accounts. Writer Kennedy Fraser described this state well, as she explained the tremendous urgency with which she, too, sought nonfiction (emphasis mine):

> For several years in my early thirties, I would sit in my arm-chair reading books about these other lives. Sometimes when I came to the end, I would sit down and read the book through from the beginning again. I remember an incredible intensity about all this, and also a kind of furtiveness—as if I were afraid that someone might look through the window and find me out. Even now, I feel I should pretend that I was reading only these women's fiction or their poetry—their lives as they chose to present them, alchemized as art. But that would be a lie. *It was the private messages I really liked—the journals and letters, and autobiographies and biographies whenever they seemed to be telling the truth.* I felt very lonely then, self-absorbed, shut off. I needed all this murmured chorus, this continuum of true-life stories, to pull me through. They were like mothers and sisters to me, these literary women, many of them already dead; more than my own family, they seemed to stretch out a hand. . . . The successes gave me hope, of course, yet it was the desperate bits I liked best. I was looking for directions, gathering clues. . . . Honest personal writing is a great service rendered the living. . . . [We] read hungrily about the lives of others, for the consolation of knowing that whatever [we] have experienced and felt, they had experienced and felt as well.

Certainly fiction accomplishes consolation and validation like the above. But it does so by different means, and its effects reverberate differently. The difference has something to do with the memoir's assumed authenticity—which detractors criticize as involving less art to make, and less to apprehend. Writer Anna

Quindlen cites the memoir's "luster of instant veracity . . . in a world in which everyone seems to lie to everyone else." Memoirs may galvanize our imaginations precisely because of their quick accessibility. The first person voice, Paul Auster has said, "goes straight into your skull," piercing awareness with the powerful intimacy of the speaker's lips at your ear. But why must easy entrée automatically cheapen the treasures discovered? Are some kinds of rapture or redemptive ease not merited unless we have hunted hard enough for them?

A somewhat more troublesome charge against the memoir form in America is that of its ostensible narcissism. Writer/editor Phyllis Rose summarizes it this way: "It's invidious, says the grumpy elitist, to put the formation of self at the center of the literary enterprise. It's possible to feel that Americans have been trained—who knows how?—to be too quick on the draw with the story of their lives. . . . Maybe personal narrative has too much of a sway in our culture."

Rose's rebuttal? That the best memoir transcends narcissism, "confronting history, directed outward"; that it issues "from the social side of human nature," endeavoring to make sense of the whole by studying its relation to the small part—that the memoirist's impulse is "to preserve herself by giving herself away." I would add that the offering of testimony, of bearing witness as a way of giving shape to history of all kinds (cultural, national, familial), derives from a long and strangely pure, still unassailable tradition that compels us instantly. We rarely think to associate the testament of a witness with mere selfishness or narcissism— we might even argue it forms the premise for the existence of a narrative voice in all literature: "I alone have escaped to tell thee." The arena silences, awaiting the story.

Many readers admit passing through phases of immersion in the memoir and in comparable nonfiction forms. And if these seekers later fan out or move on to a greater preoccupation with fiction, they seldom abandon the memoir, nor regret time given to it, regarding it simply as another form of nourishment. We attend what is called the actual with different expectations, a different musculature of perception—closer perhaps to that which we bring to reading history. But to brand autobiographical literature as "slighter" eclipses its contribution. Perhaps my point can best be made in the negative. If the present body of admired literature were suddenly stripped of all memoiristic work, and all future such work forbidden, would the loss to human art be great? The answer from my own life's experience must be: absolutely.

I think about the form as I read Maxim Gorky's classic *My Childhood,* an account of his early, hard years growing up in a Russian village with his grandparents. Painfully beautiful, it spreads a tableau of brutally difficult life seen from the wondering child's eyes, in the manner of Isaac Babel, I. B. Singer, James Agee, or Harper Lee. Work like Gorky's, or Vladimir Nabokov's exquisite *Speak, Memory,* which appears to dwell midway in the membrane between fiction and nonfiction—the kind I like best—has long troubled purists. The story, voice, and prose are numinous; yet we hesitate to ascribe it full artistic weight.

Lorrie Moore teased that ambiguous line in a story some years back, an electrifying account of a writer's ordeal with her infant son's cancer. In each thorn-sharp detail we believe the story to be Moore's own: from her description of the tiny gobbet of blood in the baby's diaper, to the maddening nonchalance of the attending physicians, to her protagonist's refusal to write the experience in memoir form as a corruption of her usual art (fiction)—to her terrible need, facing medical bills, for the money the story's sale will bring. Then mischievously, as if to set the story spinning like a top to blur its boundaries and riddle our perception, the magazine announced the piece as fiction.

Often the odder or more obscure the work, the more piercingly it may lodge in memory. I recall like tenderest old friends E. B. White's personal essays, Joel Agee's *Twelve Years* (which author James Lardner called "so beautiful, you can't own too many editions of it"), Annie Dillard's *An American Childhood,* Richard Rhodes' *A Hole in the World,* Paul Auster's *The Invention of Solitude,* James Merrill's *A Different Person,* Mary McCarthy's *Memories of a Catholic Girlhood,* Bernard Cooper's *Maps to Anywhere,*

Primo Levi's *Moments of Reprieve,* and John McGahern's exquisite *All Will Be Well.* The women are legion—think of Maya Angelou, Eudora Welty, Virginia Woolf, Isak Dinesen, or May Sarton, whose many autobiographical works (whatever else may be said about them) have, per the late Carolyn Heilbrun, "done a lot of work in the world." Each reader's list of favorites reads like part of a resumé naming influences—natures that illuminated, shaped, or fed our own. The best of these seem to charge us with something of the writer's spirit, and inasmuch as anyone may still allow for the notion, something of her soul.

Writers reach for their material by recollection as well as by imagining (both modes investigate), and form is finally no one else's to prescribe. In fact, writers know each work tends to suggest its own form. Each form confers certain advantages and limits. And while the memoir form may ultimately be judged incomplete, it may yet open a keyhole view of new territory; may shed light, ventilate, fit a missing piece to our vision of the world. Like all compelling literature, memoirs can seem at once to be happening within us and *to* us; another's life slipped momentarily over our own, an imposed yet familiar dream.

How? By attaching reader identification to recognizable thoughts, emotions, actions, or events, and thence into the unfamiliar—segueing from known to unknown, concatenating belief through successive experiences like stitches through knitting. We may remember the early pleasures of light and food and music, or the stomach-knotting dread of quarrels between parents, but have not likely sailed from New York to East Germany to live (Joel Agee), worked in the hold of a freighter bound for Alaska (E. B. White), or grown up in the bosom of a stern black nanny in a southern town (Lillian Hellman). As the writers' perceptions seep into ours, so do their revelations and sorrows.

Carolyn Heilbrun made a case for first-person nonfiction as communion with "unmet friends," people whose stories so profoundly enter and affect us that we feel thereafter personally in their debt. I know that when I look up from each succeeding chapter of Gorky I am fundamentally changed, chastened by a terrible beauty, whether depicted in the vision of a frozen corpse with its throat cut, or a summer night's descent:

> There were sunsets, when what looked like rivers of flame ran down the sky, and golden cinders seemed to shower down on the garden's velvet green. Everything grew a shade deeper in hue, and a size larger, to swell out in the warm, enfolding dusk. Weary of the sun, the leaves hung limp, the grass was bowed, everything softened and mellowed, and gave forth gentle, fragrant exhalations that calmed like music. And music, itself, in fitful gusts, was wafted in from peasants or picnickers in the fields.
>
> Night fell. . . . [T]he stillness stroked the heart, and . . . all the bitterness and dirt of the day, was scraped away. To lie with one's face upturned to the sky, to watch the stars burning in its infinite deeps, each high range opening upon a new, starry vista, was entrancing. . . . And the dark and the stillness deepened, with every instant; yet sounds followed one another, tiny, drawn out, barely audible; each, whether it be a bird drowsily chirping in its sleep, or a hedgehog running, or a subdued human voice, different from its daytime sound, had something individual that lovingly accentuated the sentient stillness.

Writer and teacher Fenton Johnson reminds us that because all memory is patchy, the best memoirists conjure artful ("the key word is 'artful'") ways to alert us that they are spinning connective tissue. "What's at issue is not the relative value of fiction and nonfiction," Johnson notes, "but the writer's signed-in-blood moral responsibility to keep the readers posted as to the workings of his particular memory. As with photojournalism and art photography, the genres of fiction and memoir serve different ends."

Suppose we viewed the path of modern letters with the same curiosity and cheerful fatalism with which we follow the development of modern music: none of the masters threatened; new energy acknowledged for its bravado. Somewhere at about mid-ribcage we know that true artistic measure can't be taken until much, much later. What does not abide, in any form, will fall away. Thus, when individuals excoriate the memoir movement as mostly awful work emerging under the auspices of literary purpose, I'd cheerfully answer—as people do, in response to complaints of bad weather—simply, "wait."

If You Really
Want to Hear
About It

In my alternate life as a book reviewer, I come across a practice that's more and more pervasive, and it happens like this:

A first novel by a very bright, up-and-coming young author arrives for review. At the back of the novel the publisher has attached a section called (I'll invent a title to camouflage it) "Additional Info and More About Me."

This section features the writer's photo—way handsome—followed by a little snack tray of personal chat: a self-deprecating, witty narrative about his life, background, the writing of the book, and a quick tour of the books he's presently reading. For a farewell flourish he lists all the titles he'd first wanted to give this novel, and his funny reasons for rejecting each.

The purpose of these sparkling riffs is of course to draw readers. The "More About Me" section—promised in a shiny, medal-like sticker on the book's cover—offers a literary *amuse-bouche.*

Of course I skip straight to this section, the same way I leaf through gossip magazines at the supermarket checkout. And in an instant, I want to tell the writer (and his publicist) with a groan: *No, no, no. Please don't do this.*

It isn't that the author's small talk isn't fun or tasteful—it's downright demure, compared with the circus antics of many websites and trailers. But a website or a video trailer—so far anyhow—exists in a separate physical (or virtual) space. If you make a sandwich of the actual novel slapped up against the author's jolly scrapbook noodling, it strikes me that you not only devalue the novel—you make it almost irrelevant. Why should a reader bother with a flimsy, made-up story when she can zero in, between the same covers, on the tasty dirt of the writer's life?

My guess is that most readers will skim the novel *after* having sucked up the more salacious stuff at the back—and only then if there happens to be nothing else to do.

And there's always, always something else to do.

To survive, literary fiction—last time I checked—must create urgency, even inside the quietest tale. A reader's got to need to push through, compelled by the *story's* voice, or because she's curious about what happens next, or both. She's got to care. One of the lines that still reverberates across decades is Holden Caulfield's tense refrain: *If you really want to hear about it. . . .* Those words served as Holden's sword and shield—and bait. Very few, he understood, really give a toss. It's a story's job to lure them.

I'm not arguing for piousness, exactly. I like the junk food of gossip as much as anybody, and to be fair, artists' personal struggles (when we read their letters, for example) can inspire as powerfully as their works. Just, please—evoking that famous old *New Yorker* division between its advertising and editorial departments—can't we keep the elevator doors separate?

A writer offers a piece of fiction by way of saying *Here is a dream I made.* The reader takes it into her hands, answering *I accept your dream for the duration of its reading—if it can hold me.* The dream is a world. Unlike a website, film, or television show, a book doesn't commend itself to dreams when bound together with a series of outtakes, commercial tie-ins, funny bloopers, action figures, key chains, and the author tweeting what he ate for breakfast. Those latter forms of outfall may show up—but please, don't leash them to the art.

Introductions and acknowledgment pages aside—when personality profiling is packed cheek to cheek with fiction, it strikes me that the primacy of the "real" voice nearly always trumps. Some delicate membrane dissolves, a little sickeningly. Readers' sympathies naturally flow toward the "actual"—melting fiction's dream, rendering it gossamer, sometimes even silly. What's more, a reader can sneak back anytime and check out those dishy pages whenever she gets bored with the story (the poor story!)—like porn stashed in the back of a textbook.

So when that delicious suspension—*okay, for this moment, this dream and no other*—is punctured, what's left? The novel becomes an infomercial or larky exercise, winking the neon message *Ha, Just Fooling Around.*

A new genre? Possibly. And for some that might be ideal—but I can't really say I want to hear about it. There's little time, and so much wonderful work out there yet to read.

In Search of
Heated Agreement

How are we to spend our lives,
anyway? . . . We read to seek the
answer, and the search itself—the
task of a lifetime—becomes the answer.
　　　　—Lynne Sharon Schwartz,
　　　　　　　Ruined by Reading

We were wolfing Greek olives and crackers, preludes to the good dinner she and her husband were preparing, when a friend announced to me:

"I ordered a half dozen of those books you recommended, and I didn't like any of them."

I stared at my hostess, an amiable and whip-smart memoirist. My face went warm; the olives and crackers in my mouth turned to glue. I could not remember, in that instant, which books I'd told her to read. Doubtless they'd represented some of my "best marbles," works I'd found thrilling, even life-changing.

In the next beat I knew it didn't matter. What would it serve to bring up those titles one by one, cross-examine her about exactly why she'd hated them? How would I rebut her findings?

I'd heard too many such conversations:

"The story was unbelievable, the characters too distanced. I didn't care about them."

"But that's not true. The story was fresh, important. I'll never forget it."

"The story was silly." (Uttered reprovingly, fondly: *Come now. We both understand you know better.*)

Things accelerate. Sooner or later the glove is flung:

"I hate historical fiction (magical realism, fiction set in academia, epistemological fiction, etc.)."

"How can you say that? I love historical fiction!"

And on it goes, each side interjecting with louder grandiloquence, as if decibels gave a moral edge. The talk could be about the merits of okra or beets—except one doesn't tend to hold it against one's closest friends for hating beets.

Everyone's well-spoken. Yet nothing more complicated is proposed, over and over, than *I am right about this, and you are wrong.* Each side ultimately defaults to the irreducible *Because I see it that way.* No one has been persuaded of anything when the swords are dropped—but each side has taken private, sad note of her opponent's astonishing shortsightedness, perhaps also her insensitivity. Though they continue to smile at each other, each friend has fallen a notch, forever, in the other's secret esteem.

I swallowed with difficulty after my hostess buttonholed me. Embarrassment was what I felt, along with a powerful wish to disappear—or at least change the subject before dinner. I managed it, I think, but not before she had strapped down her indictment a different way:

"You always seem to prefer cerebral books."

Oh, dear. As if the category were a cold, smoking liquid poured from laboratory beakers. How to respond? In fact I knew well enough what my hostess meant. She meant that I liked writing that (to her) felt inaccessible, turgid, bloodless, antilife. *Cerebral* was a euphemism, deployed to sound respectful in place of her private creed about writing—that common sense trumps erudition every time, and that examples of each camp were as readily identifiable as, well, okra or beets.

Horrified, I nodded, murmured. I'd been slapped with an identification badge no comeback could modify. Any protest would sink me further. Best to stay quiet, slink away. Let her win by virtue of my speechlessness.

Make no mistake, though: my heart registered this event in the small but clean, well-lit war room at its center. A map is spread out there, colorful pins stuck in it: here the hostile camps, there the safe harbors. Instructions from that quarter issued at once, by hotline: *Never again urge any book you truly love and believe in upon this person. Never expect her to understand.*

Sad? To me, oh, yes. Very sad.

But most of the time, inevitable.

The subjectivity of literary taste is a democratic thing. My own husband shrugs at writers I follow fervently. They just don't reach him that way. I gave an extremely bright, well-read friend a title I consider a dusky treasure: *A Month in the Country* by J. L. Carr, the brief, lovely novel about a shell-shocked soldier from the First World War finding bittersweet solace in the restoration of a country church. She reported she could not stand it. I gave William Maxwell's exquisite *So Long, See You Tomorrow* (a wrenching story of remembered friendship, the early loss of a mother, a doomed, adulterous love, and consequent murder) to the wife of a colleague of my husband, for her book group. It depressed her. She put it aside. You might argue I'm picking the wrong friends or even the wrong husband, but the phenomenon's much more democratic than that. I still remember mailing Shirley Hazzard's brilliant novel of the lives of two extraordinary sisters in mid-century England, *The Transit of Venus,* to my late best friend, who was among the most insightful readers I may ever know. Deborah e-mailed her verdict: she admired the work at the outset, but her interest cooled midway. Such responses shock me when they arrive; I must retreat somewhere alone to tremble and gather my wits. It is difficult to listen to the particulars of a loved one's dislike—not only because the relationship at stake is primary, but because my relationship to the *book* is primary.

There's no way to deny it: The disappointment feels moral, a personal affront. The book in question was a test, and he/she failed it. The book was a symbol of a singular, essential awareness: he/she missed it entirely, or repudiated that awareness out of hand. And while I can admit to the logic of some objections (a subtle piousness infiltrates *A Month in the Country*, and the second half of *Venus* does not perhaps pack the same wallop as the first)—I don't want to give those objections much airtime. Damn the minor weaknesses; the work's spirit (voice, gesture) is what matters—and deserves to be cherished.

One prefers to keep one's husband. One hopes to go on seeing one's friends. But something inside remains punctured in the private wake of a rejected book. The mind murmurs ever after in their company: *Take caution. Be on guard with this person. It wasn't quite as you supposed.*

In the words of a Charles Baxter character—fuck and alas.

I used to believe that my lonely exasperation with opposing (or indifferent) literary tastes simply meant I'd become an old-fashioned crank. Time and again I've admonished myself that my convictions about books have grown so uncompromising, so proprietary, so fierce that there is almost no sense anymore trying to talk about them with people—the effort will likely drive me, and probably them, crazy. If I persist in trying, I face responses like that of my dinner hostess—or that of the young writer I met at an art colony, who brightly hailed a passing composer, dashing away to chat with him as I was in hopeful mid-sentence beside her: "So I'm reading this new Doris Lessing—." (It was *The Grandmothers*, a quartet of novellas; what had speared me through the ribs was the last of the four, a wartime story of love briefly found and repudiated, called *The Love Child*.) Apparently I lack normal defenses— no mitigating, protective skin, and no prospects of growing one. In fact the reverse feels true. The older I get the more unequivocal (and therefore vulnerable) I feel about various titles, what they hold, what they promise, and what they deliver. When I ask a writing class, "Have any of you heard of Mavis Gallant?" and look out on a sea of vacant, impassive faces (though they are young, for heaven's sake), it leaves me confounded, and vaguely shamed. Anyone else, I reason, would not take the matter so personally. Two selves go to war then. One hisses: *Suck it up. Be a big girl. No one promised you heated agreement, even inside art colonies.* The other wails like a bereft baby: *But this is the most important thing there is. This is where the treasure is buried.*

Paula Fox, in an essay on language, quotes this sentence from Carol Bly's praise of a Conrad Aiken story: "If we hadn't had his story, and others like it, *we might never recognize how dear we hold our private perception of the universe.*"

I have read that sentence again and again.

If I could swap out this soggy emotional baggage for some crisp armor, believe me, I would do it in a stroke. And if you're skimming these words toward some tidy resolution—I'm sorry. To live and work in contemporary culture is, in the main, to be forced to bury one's literary passions like a creepy sexual habit. That may come as no surprise to those of us who make our livings at day jobs in the worlds of commerce, where books and reading figure almost not at all, exempting *TV Guide* and trendy beach reads. But what *does* surprise is that even among artists and writers (and this realization mauled what may have been the last stronghold of my own naïveté), odds for connection can prove little better. Odds would, on the surface, seem terrific for it. Yet I have learned over the years that artists tend to be a guarded lot, by long habit. Pleasant at best, nasty at not so best, they are often distracted with the business of shepherding their own work toward visibility. Or they defend instinctively against various forms of importuning as another intrusive energy drain, living at a remove, a deliberate exile that for mysterious reasons refuses to be broached. Edna O'Brien once remarked that writers were indeed lonely people, "seldom meet[ing] their match in life, or in each other, though on state occasions purporting to!" The reason, O'Brien said, is simple: "They do not want to. The intimacy so longed for has to be forever deferred." In that thumbnail cameo, of course, I recognize myself. Some part of the writer must stand away, forever outside looking in: it is Tonio Kröger—needy, irritable—who makes art; seldom the jolly, sated burgher. I too generate this push-pull, this sticky force field. Paradoxically, though, the *pull* factor never yields. We need to feel the other's comprehension, feel it enter him the way it entered us. So we ask, always against better knowledge, *What are you reading?* Against logic we seek the light in the eye, the tone of voice that "on state occasion" brings relief so acute it feels almost like pain. Its message? *Yes. I know exactly what you mean.*

❚   ❚   ❚

The night of my hostess's dinner party, our respective husbands set up a small commotion on the subject of Zadie Smith. No matter that the media was already saturated, at the time, with every possible pronouncement—the men went at it, fencing along lines described above. "Oh, you're wrong. She's this." "No, not at all: she's that." And up it loomed again: that big, dumb impasse between contenders, each of them swinging at air. It was a Monty Python scene: words inanimate and limp, rubber chickens lobbed over castle walls. Were these men, or the rest of us (waiting quietly with our drinks) even slightly moved by their jousting? Not a bit. The point, it seemed, was to wedge in a last word, and to do it with panache—often, I suppose, that is the human sum of nearly everything, the impulse to sound good to oneself, to others. Similar gridlock occurs in talk of films or plays. Lines are drawn, ranks closed, interpenetration rare. "It was life-affirming." "Nonsense. It was sappy."

Unfairly, I still crave the kind of discourse relished with my late best friend. (Even though she disappointed me with her response to the Hazzard title and a few others, there was a rich enough history of dialogue between us to absorb many differences.) Our discussions, mostly by e-mail in final years, were earnest. I could consider her arguments without rancor because her ideas were suggested with intelligence and feeling. I could affirm which of them felt valid, and counter those which struck me as incomplete or flawed. To be honest, I doubt that either of us ever persuaded the other of a blessed thing. We liked the sound of ourselves. Yet we both felt provoked and deepened, I think, by the back and forth of it. She knew the importance of the search, in our reading, for what we called *the next It of Its:* the book that would smash prior records, crack open our minds and hearts with the power of Apollo's archaic torso. Closely related to that ideal was another favorite motto: *Never relinquish the Quest plot*—alluding not to the books we read, but to our lives' pursuit of them.

Now I look about, and notice that civilized literary conversation carries similar tensions, even among our biggest guns. Hazzard's novel of the Second World War, *The Great Fire,* won the National Book Award, yet British author John Banville took severe exception to that work in a *New York Times* vivisection. Banville himself was awarded the Booker Prize for his novel (of remembrance and class in Ireland), *The Sea,* amid a well-publicized storm of dissent, including a flaying by the *New York Times'* Michiko Kakutani. Certain Nobel jurists, many will recall, resigned several years ago in furious protest over their committee's selection for the fiction prize.

How dear we hold our private perception of the universe. Perhaps the dinner party, for all its crude noise, is an accurate microcosm.

Reviewers are usually themselves writers, equipped with their own biases, their own force fields. Things get tricky when someone whose work we admire singles a book out—let's make up a title, say, *The Many-Layered Cake*—in a review, praising it emphatically. At once we think, thrilled, greedy, Yes! Onto my list it goes! And off we march to find *The Many-Layered Cake*—just out in trade paper as it happens; what a boon. We race it home and lo: the book takes form as a series of journal entries, not at all to our liking; the language is hyperclever, dense, annoying. We lug it back to the store. Next time, we remind ourselves angrily, we will not be in such an all-fired hurry. Thank heaven our local book vendor gives in-store credit. But now we are stuck with a new frustration, that of the overpacked memory: What was the name of that infernal writer-reviewer who praised the book? Because we'll have to approach his future evaluations with caution now. And again we grow conscious of an insidious prickling. Someone we thought we could trust has let us down.

A kinder and (inherently) more joyful vision of this impasse may be found in a passage from the gorgeous recent translation, by Richard Pevear and Larissa Volokhonsky, of *Anna Karenina*. Italics and bolded italics are mine:

> Levin had often noticed in arguments between the most intelligent people that after enormous efforts, an enormous number of logical subtleties and words, the arguers would finally come to the awareness that what they had spent so long struggling to prove to each other *had been known to them long, long before, from the beginning of the argument,* **but that they loved different things and therefore did not want to name what they loved, so as not to be challenged.** He had often felt that sometimes during an argument you would understand what your opponent loves, and suddenly come to love the same thing yourself, and agree all at once, and then all reasonings would fall away as superfluous; and sometimes it was the other way round: you would finally say what you yourself love, for the sake of which you are inventing your reasonings, and if you happened to say it well and sincerely, the opponent would suddenly agree and stop arguing.

Yet the appetite for heated agreement, like other appetites, regenerates. One carries on against ruinous odds, praying to be met—think of a strong handshake with both hands—by someone who shares a crank's passion, or at least comprehends its source. The question *what are you reading*, still seized upon at once by believers, shivers in my ears with pent-up thrall: What news, what star, what map have you found? Tell me yours; I'll tell you mine! Lamp held aloft, I hobble on, taking my private little census wherever the least glint of potential receptivity winks at me. Have you read, I ask. Have you heard of. Do you know. Try this, I say, foisting yet another copy of *So Long, See You Tomorrow* (and too many other titles to list here) on the hapless new mark. It's doleful, quixotic folly. Yet I cannot help believing the mind always exists out there, skulking along in a matching state of complicated, imperious yearning. It need not—truly it needn't—be a mirror reflection of my own. It need only share the condition (like a high fever) of loving certain titles as if they were holy, kept near for their numinous power, and the understanding that at bottom there is nothing more important than the search for the next quiet miracle in the sacred underground stream of beautiful, disturbing, abiding work, whose mysterious voice whispers *here is something true.*

Making Art

Love of Three Oranges

*Do your work honestly and truthfully,
and keep the work in your mind, and
your loved ones.*

—Grace Paley

What does it mean to declare oneself a member of the shape-shifting, embattled fraternity of artists?

What does being an artist truly mean or require?

To some, the definition's clear-cut. You do your art as hard as you can, any way you can, as much of your waking life as you can. Nothing else matters—including, if necessary, food, shelter, sleep. Secondary survival—love, community, well-being—may not even figure.

The art, say the above believers, is all.

To most others, a life of making art means a lifetime of complex, difficult compromise. It means re-choosing at every turn to juggle art alongside survival and love—three oranges, if you will, grasped in rapid succession (sometimes two at a clutch): now the love, now the labors of subsistence, now the art.

"It's interesting," deadpanned the late, beloved Grace Paley at a reading, when an audience member asked plaintively how she managed it. There is, too, the rather fiendish artistic reason for keeping life and love close at hand (besides the utterly human need for these) which may not at first seem obvious: material. The artist draws constantly (some would say ruthlessly) from life for her work's marrow—infusing it with the soul-energy which illuminates and animates it. "I would give a pint of my own blood [for a good story]," an author I admire told a class calmly one day.

It appears to me that the large majority of working writers— who've observed some history—have decided that it serves neither art nor life to die for art. By that, I mean they decline to make sacrifices that will destroy them. These may include forgoing food, sleep, shelter, abusing substances—or so ostracizing yourself from human connection that the soul atrophies, and the body follows. If you die for art you cannot do art. Blackout.

Artists, or people who study and teach great works of art, may argue about what makes art great, and what sort of regimen defines the "purest" or most dedicated artist. On its face, the former exertion strikes me as an inevitable, ongoing dialectic—the latter, an invitation to disaster. My late best friend was much taken with this latter exercise, a sort of Who's The Fairest of Them All guessing game, and I argued with her about the wastefulness of it. Who can finally say with certainty what the notion of sacrifice really entails, and how much it determines any quality of art? Are they connected at all?

Here's what she offered, cautioning that it was purely her conjecture:

> A work does not become great by means of sacrifice, but a work might be allowed greatness by means of sacrifice. . . . "Sacrifice" can include, but is not limited to, doing without children, spouse, medical insurance, air conditioning, car, vitamins, three meals a day, sleep, health, videotaped episodes of *As The World Turns,* or a sense of well-being. It's probably possible to achieve great art without sacrificing any of the

above if all of the above are provided or tended to by spouse, sibling, state, parent, or lottery win.

Also, I am defining "greatness" in the usual daunting sense of the word. Henry James, Dostoevsky, Eliot, and company. It is the achievement of the few. Some achieve good art. More achieve competent art. Many achieve mediocre art. And most achieve bad art. As you have reminded me again and again, we can't be overwhelmed by the idea of greatness or we'd go out and eat dirt.

I sense that what my friend most deeply intended, in her thinking about sacrifice, was the idea of undertaking a venture that risks at soul-level. That is, to push off in the making of the work without sight of the opposite shore, without promise of acknowledgment, reward, or safety. "The axe to the frozen sea within us" swings not just toward the complacency of art's witnesses but also back at the maker, toward the artist's own complacency at multiple levels. You're in the act of cracking out, cracking open, drawing your own blood. This stance may be accused of romanticism. But I believe Kafka's right, if we mean to make art that matters.

Nonetheless, this same friend brought me up short when she next asked, quite innocently: "How much great art can you think of that has been created in the margins?"

Speechlessness.

Blank screen.

Instant shame.

Not one example, not one pale snippet of evidence could I immediately conceive—though someone later pointed out that Wallace Stevens was an insurance lawyer, Dostoevsky a degenerate gambler, Williams a doctor, Eliot a bank officer. (Still later, I remembered Robert Olen Butler wrote on the subway ride to work, Toni Morrison after her two young sons were put to bed, Jane Smiley while her kids raced in and out of her studio, and so on.) In any case, the moment my friend uttered it, the indictment sliced down with rushing finality: I have consecrated my entire adult writing life to squeezing art into the margins. Writing in stolen moments at work, at night, weekends, on the bus, between chores and guests, trips and illnesses; fragmented, distracted, exhausted.

Not good enough, by the most fundamental definition.

Not the real thing. Not a fully committed artist. Instead, a cowardly one. Half-baked. A timid equivocator.

Everyone who is really a writer, the intimation goes, is doing it during their lives' best, clearest hours. At whatever cost. Or so it seemed in the frantic moments following my friend's innocent query—moments that felt like free fall.

Here was a queer reversal: where I had thrown the weight of heroism onto the feat of effecting art around the duties of quotidian life—the Good Fight; the Righteous Underground—it had suddenly been revealed to me (so simply!) to be the opposite case. True heroism lay in making art during real time, the livelong day. Come what may.

Twyla Tharp's dance troupe, I suddenly recalled reading somewhere, went through a period, during its impoverished beginnings, of living on a single small container of yogurt, per individual, per day.

My God, I thought. I've predicated an entire book on the art of squeezing. How can I believe my work should aim for real-time consideration if it has been hammered out in haste and fatigue and distress, in the narrow gutters of real time?

I spent a sleepless night with it.

The logic seemed clear. Even putting aside the hopelessly floppy notion of greatness, by the most genial interpretation of my friend's observation I was less than a dilettante. In the same breath there was no escaping the fact—literally, with each breath—writing is what I do. I think of the aging actress Viveca Lindfors in the Henry Jaglom film *Last Summer in the Hamptons,* who burst into tears when someone asked why she was an actor: "It's what I was born to," she wept.

I unpacked all my reasoning and began again.

Few writers can live on sales of their work. Some can, but they're rare. The rest make arrangements. They teach or edit or proofread or write technical manuals or screenplays. Or they're farmers like Jane Hamilton, or surgeons like Lewis Thomas, or (former) waitresses like Heidi Julavitz. They are secretaries, house-cleaners, clerks, tennis instructors, real estate appraisers, landscape gardeners. They are kept spouses. (Sometimes they are sociopaths, co-opters of totalitarian regimes, wastrels.) Does this make them less serious as artists? Charles Baxter once called the problem of supporting your art "the nightmare from which most of us are trying to wake up." He declared it did not matter what you did to put food on the table so long as you found a way to get your art made. And what choice has a modern writer, anyway? You do it because you have to.

It may be true, as my friend has suggested by inference, that those who've consecrated their lives to it (prime-time hours) have made the best art.

It is certainly true that one can live on less.

Likewise, that each of us has unique conditions.

Arf, arf. Barking and scratching.

I am willing to admit that I complain when it all becomes too much for me, and that it's not pretty. In fact this book might be read as one long howl: *It's hard, no one's helping, society abhors it (until you succeed commercially, and then it misunderstands it), other writers clam up about it, I'm having to resort to crime and duplicity and run like a polygamous husband between life and art, income and writing, and everything suffers in the bargain.* It might even be argued that the writer striving to get work made in the margins is destroying herself more vigorously than the writer who's starving and penniless. Because the marginalist's chief energies, and perhaps too much of her spirit, are given over to stealth tactics: resistance, subterfuge, hiding, smuggling. These efforts bleed attention and clarity that might—might—have poured into the work itself. You could propose that my gesture, my song over the last twenty-some years, has been that single long yelp of pain, whilst hitting myself on the head with a hammer. I chose this, this living with too many elements in the set. Chose it and continue to choose it. I could change. I could stop. Instead I am grabbing people by the lapels, demanding—what? Comprehension? (I could dress it up and claim I am demanding art be given its rich due in the social fabric. But let's face it, I'm mainly yelling.) What logical response can anyone make?

One: You poor thing. What a terrible world, to allow this.

Two: Stop hitting yourself on the head with that hammer, you perfect fool!

Questions about artistic life must ultimately invoke those ancient and venerable human mysteries, meaning and its allocation—and their facilitating arm, human imagination.

I once asked a high-powered consultant to the software publishing firm where I then worked, what he knew for sure. It was corny, unattractive slang, a lazy greeting young people used at the time, a version of high-fiving or, later, *wassup?* Because Barry was significantly older than the rest of us, because he carried himself quietly, I flung the salutation at him one morning like a glass of ice water.

Hey, Barry! What do you know for sure?

Barry turned toward me, gazed into my eyes, and waited a voluptuous beat before answering slowly and carefully:

"That everything is exactly what you hold it to be."

I've been digesting those words for years.

The miracle of human belief.

Meaning exists as we ascribe it. It is there when we say it, as the late, gentle William Stafford reminds us in his wonderful "Farther Than Stout Cortez," (a poem to keep handy all your life):

> What almost fails
> to be in the world comes in—what fell
> through the sky, or hid in the ordinary or
> under or behind. It is there when we say it.

Of course no one can name a best way to make best art. If I let myself be drawn into the pastime of labeling and arranging levels of artistic greatness, I'd have even less time. I'm convinced that it should not fall to the artist to dwell on such questions (except maybe in terms of craft analysis). Because they (such questions) have the capacity to paralyze. Art's measure is rarely taken accurately in its own time, but never mind. Let the critics knock themselves out measuring and pronouncing. The artist's preoccupied. She's a carpenter whose focus must be on fitting the glass smoothly into the building's frame. If she works at noon or at midnight, if she eats bananas or steak or cat food, that's her business. Her purpose is to seamlessly fit that glass.

Even if the whole structure turns to sand in fifty years. Thirty years. Five.

Do you recall the wind-up doll sayings of decades ago? You wind up the artist: she returns to the task.

We write to investigate, attend, witness. If my method involves harvesting the energy of resistance, well, that's one method. Given the nature of modern tolerance for the declared artist, perhaps some of what I've offered in these pages can provide a clue. Or cue. Thaisa Frank has written:

> How do you declare yourself a writer? You just do, like taking a big step forward. There's no need to defend yourself or tell people how you work or even what you're working on. Some writers are marathon runners and need to work every day. Others are sprinters, who germinate in silence and finish a novel in six months. If someone asks, "Really? And do you write every day?" all you have to say is, "I work until the story gets done." Lawyers don't have to defend their work habits. Neither do zookeepers. Writers don't either—even when they aren't published. Being a writer simply means that you have a passion for writing bound up with the way you think, feel, and live and that you find ways—even if serendipitous, mad, or chaotic—to honor that passion.

When even the biggest literary names make victorious reading tours, they often admit how unhappy they feel until they have settled into the next writing project—how hungrily they miss working on something, amid whatever acclaim. I believe them. The itch, the yearning, the glimpse of the next tantalizing, disturbing idea—how can I broach it, shape it, solve the inescapable problems? Where might I take it; more accurately, more excitingly, where might it take me? The call of the dream: getting back to it, getting it down. Product is good, but process, we learn the hard way, is the real, tugging star. One following onto the next, a whole sparkling cosmos of them.

Sources

This section includes source information for quotes and paraphrases that did not have the source information included with the quote or paraphrase in the text. Thaisa Frank's quotes are comments made during classes she taught that were taken by Joan Frank.

Getting It Down

Sven Birkerts's words are paraphrased from his book *The Gutenberg Elegies: The Fate of Reading in an Electronic Age* (Faber and Faber, 1994).

Jane Hamilton's description and Heidi Julavits' quotes are from *Artists' Communities*, 2nd ed. (Allworth Press, 2000).

Anne Lamott's comment was made during a writing workshop of hers that was attended by Joan Frank.

Spit and Band-Aids: The Business of Art

Saul Bellow's quote is from a letter to Susan Glassman published in the book *Saul Bellow: Letters* edited by Benjamin Taylor (New York: Viking, 2010).

The description of Saul Bellow in his letters was written by Michiko Kakutani in the *New York Times Book Review* (Nov. 8, 2010).

Katherine Anne Porter's quotes are from "The Art of Fiction No. 29," an interview by Barbara Thompson Davis in the *Paris Review* (Winter–Spring 1963).

The Stillness of Sleeping Birds

Lynne Sharon Schwartz's quotes are from her book *Ruined by Reading: A Life in Books* (Beacon Press, 1996).

Sven Birkerts's words are paraphrased from his book *The Gutenberg Elegies: The Fate of Reading in an Electronic Age* (Faber and Faber, 1994).

Francine Prose's remark was made at a discussion sponsored by City Arts & Lectures in San Francisco, CA.

Gail Godwin's quote is from her essay "The Watcher at the Gate."

Charles Baxter's quotes are from the essay "Stillness" in his book *Burning Down the House: Essays on Fiction* (Graywolf Press, 1997).

Raymond Chandler's quote is from his essay "A Qualified Farewell," which is included with several other essays in *The Notebooks of Raymond Chandler and English Summer: A Gothic Romance*, edited by Frank MacShane (Ecco Press, 1976).

Be Careful Whom You Tell

James Joyce's quote is from his book *A Portrait of the Artist as a Young Man*.

Anne Lamott refers to the diabolical radio station in her book *Bird by Bird: Some Instructions on Writing and Life.*

Never Enough

Jane Austen's quote is from her book *Pride and Prejudice.*

Ann Richards's quote in part 99 appeared in Pamela Stone's book *A Women's Guide to Living Alone: 10 Ways to Survive Grief and Be Happy* (Taylor Trade, 2001).

The poetry quote in part 172 is from the Wallace Stevens poem "Gubbinal," which is included in Stevens's poetry collection *Harmonium.*

Writers' Networks, Writers' Lives

Mary McCarthy's quote is from "The Art of Fiction No. 27," an interview by Elisabeth Sifton in the *Paris Review* (Winter–Spring 1962).

For My Brothers and Sisters in the Rejection Business

Margaret Edson's interview with Jim Lehrer on the PBS News-Hour aired on April 14, 1999. A transcript of the interview can be found on the PBS NewsHour website, www.pbs.org/newshour/.

Seymour Krim's essay, "For My Brothers and Sisters in the Failure Business," is included in Phillip Lopate's anthology *The Art of the Personal Essay: An Anthology from the Classical Era to the Present* (Anchor Books, 1995).

The quote from *Kirkus* was from their review of Joan Frank's book *Boys Keep Being Born,* specifically the short story "The Guardian." The review was published on Aug. 15, 2001.

Frederick Busch's quotes are from "An Interview with Frederick Busch," written by Justin Cronin for the *Writer's Chronicle* (March/April 1999).

The Impenetrable Phenomenon

Shirley Hazzard's quote was originally published in "Posillipo: A Scene of Ancient Fame," a travel piece Hazzard wrote for the *New York Times* (March 7, 1993). It has now been reprinted in "A Scene of Ancient Fame," a chapter from Shirley Hazzard and Francis Steegmuller's book *The Ancient Shore: Dispatches from Naples* (University of Chicago Press, 2008).

The Vastness of Geologic Time

Jonathan Franzen's quote is from his essay "Farther Away: 'Robinson Crusoe,' David Foster Wallace, and the island of solitude," which was published in the *New Yorker* (April 18, 2011).

The quote about the young man who had played classical guitar is from the article "How To Fail Successfully: When to give up on our ambitions? Glenn Kurtz learned the answer the hard way" by Chris Colin, special to SF Gate, www.sfgate.com, online home of the *San Francisco Chronicle* (June 8, 2007).

Mark Morris's quote is from Joan Acocella's book *Twenty-Eight Artists and Two Saints: Essays* (Vintage Books, 2008).

The More We Typed, the Better We Felt

P. G. Wodehouse's quote is from a letter of his that was featured in the "Along Publisher's Row" section of the *Authors Guild Bulletin* (Spring 2008).

Revisiting Envy

Donald's Sheehan's quotes and anecdotes are from his article "To Be Free of Envy."

René Girard's description is from his book *A Theatre of Envy.*

Bonnie Friedman's characterization of envy is from her book *Writing Past Dark: Envy, Fear, Distraction, and Other Dilemmas in the Writer's Life* (HarperCollins, 1993).

Gumby, Frankenstein, Jakob, Rosamund

Siri Hustvedt's quotes are from her book *A Plea for Eros* (Picador, 2006).

Shirley Hazzard's quote is from her essay "William Maxwell" in the book *A William Maxwell Portrait: Memories and Appreciations,* edited by Charles Baxter, Michael Collier, and Edward Hirsch (W. W. Norton & Co., 2004).

Sven Birkerts's words are paraphrased from his book *The Gutenberg Elegies: The Fate of Reading in an Electronic Age* (Faber and Faber, 1994).

James Salter's quote is from his essay "Some for Glory, Some for Praise" in the book *Why I Write: Thoughts on the Craft of Fiction,* edited by Will Blythe (Little, Brown and Company, 1998).

Striking a Bargain: Marketing

Vincent Van Gogh's letters to his brother Theo can be found in the book *The Letters of Vincent Van Gogh,* edited by Mark Roskill (Touchstone, 1997).

Dinosaurs

Paul Auster's quote is from "The Art of Austerity: Joan Frank talks to Paul Auster," an interview by Joan Frank in the *San Francisco Review of Books,* vol. 17, no. 3 (Winter 1992).

Robert Gottlieb's quote is from "From editor to writer: Legendary editor Robert Gottlieb on working with literary stars—and the miseries of his own writing process," an interview by Laura Miller for the online site Salon, www.salon.com (April 26, 2011).

Underwhelmed and Eccentric

Julien Gracq's quote is from his book *Reading Writing* (Turtle Point Press, 2006).

A Hand in the Game: Reviewing

Richard Russo's quote is from "Up Front," an article by the editors of the *New York Times Book Review* (June 1, 2008).

Richard Ford's quote is from a conversation with Nam Le at the PEN World Voices Festival on May 3, 2009. A partial transcript of this conversation, including the quote, can be found in "Richard Ford, Nam Le, in Conversation," a post by Jane Ciabattari on *Critical Mass*, the National Book Critics Circle blog, www.bookcritics.org (May 6, 2009).

John Updike's quotes are from "Reviewing 101: John Updike's Rules," a post by John Freeman on *Critical Mass*, the National Book Critics Circle blog, www.bookcritics.org (June 8, 2006).

Joe Queenan's quotes are from his essay "Enough With the Sweet Talk," published in the *New York Times Book Review* (Nov. 14, 2008).

Enough with the Change and Growth

Charles Baxter's quotes are from the essay "Against Epiphanies" in his book *Burning Down the House: Essays on Fiction* (Graywolf Press, 1997).

The quote, "when I became a man, I put away childish things," is from 1 Corinthians 13:11 (King James Bible).

The quote, "Reader, I married him," is from *Jane Eyre* by Charlotte Brontë.

The quote, "Aunt Sally, she's going to adopt me and sivilize me, and I can't stand it. I been there before," is from *The Adventures of Huckleberry Finn* by Mark Twain.

Sarah Ruhl's remark is from "Surreal Life," an article by John Lahr for the *New Yorker* (March 17, 2008).

Flannery O'Connor's quote is from the book *Mystery and Manners: Occasional Prose,* selected and edited by Sally and Robert Fitzgerald.

Elizabeth Strout's reminder that "Olive belongs to *you* now" was given to a bookstore audience at Book Passage in California.

Imposed Yet Familiar: Defending the Memoir

Ellen Goodman's quotes are from her column "What Can We Make of the Current Craving for Memoirs?" in the *Boston Globe* (April 6, 1997).

Robert Hass's quote is from "An Interview with Poet Laureate Robert Hass," written by Joan Frank for the *San Francisco Review,* vol. 21.6 (Nov./Dec. 1996).

Kennedy Fraser's quote is from her book *Ornament and Silence: Essays on Women's Lives* (Knopf, 1996).

Anna Quindlan's quote is from "How Dark? How Stormy? I Can't Recall," a "Bookend" article for the *New York Times* (May 11, 1997).

Paul Auster's quote is from "The Art of Austerity: Joan Frank talks to Paul Auster," an interview by Joan Frank in the *San Francisco Review of Books,* vol. 17, no. 3 (Winter 1992).

Phyllis Rose's quotes are from her introduction to *The Norton Book of Women's Lives,* edited by Phyllis Rose (W. W. Norton & Co., 1993).

James Lardner's quote is from a spoken conversation with Joan Frank at the MacDowell Colony in 1991.

Carolyn Heilbrun's quote, "unmet friends," is from her book *The Last Gift of Time: Life Beyond Sixty* (Dial Press, 1997).

Maxim Gorky's quote is from his work "My Childhood" in his book *Autobiography of Maxim Gorky: Three Great Works in One Volume,* translated by Isidor Schneider (Citadel Press, 1949).

Fenton Johnson's quote is from his letter to the editor, "What Happened?," in the *New York Times* (June 8, 1997).

If You Really Want to Hear About It

Holden Caulfield's tense refrain is from *The Catcher in the Rye* by J. D. Salinger.

In Search of Heated Agreement

Charles Baxter's character's words are from Baxter's book *The Feast of Love.*

Paula Fox quotes Carol Bly's praise of a Conrad Aiken story in "A Respected Author Muses on Language's Power vs. Lingo and Labels," Fox's essay for *School Library Journal* 41, no. 3 (March 1995).

Edna O'Brien's quotes are from a profile article in *More* magazine.

The quote from *Anna Karenina,* by Leo Tolstoy, is from the translation by Richard Pevear and Larissa Volokhonsky (Penguin Books, 2000).

Love of Three Oranges

Viveca Lindfors's quote is from the Hanry Jaglom film *Last Summer in the Hamptons* (1995).

William Stafford's poem, "Farther Than Stout Cortez," was published in his book *Listening Deep* (Penmaen Press, 1984).